Anne PERRY

A CHRISTMAS MESSAGE

HEADLINE

Copyright © 2016 Anne Perry

The right of Anne Perry to be identified as the Author of
the Work has been asserted by her in accordance with the
Copyright, Designs and Patents Act 1988.

First published in 2016 by
HEADLINE PUBLISHING GROUP

First published in paperback in 2017 by
HEADLINE PUBLISHING GROUP

1

Cataloguing in Publication Data is available from the British Library

ISBN 978 1 4722 3422 3

Typeset in Times New Roman PS by Palimpsest Book Production Limited,
Falkirk, Stirlingshire

Printed and bound by CPI Group (UK) Ltd, Croydon CR0 4YY

HEADLINE PUBLISHING GROUP
An Hachette UK Company
Carmelite House
50 Victoria Embankment
London EC4Y 0DZ

www.headline.co.uk
www.hachette.co.uk

To all who follow a star

Vespasia stood at the long, open window of her hotel bedroom and gazed across the rooftops of the city towards the western sky. The sun was sinking into the Mediterranean, as if it were bleeding crimson into the water. The light was fading quickly. The air was already cooler, but it was gone mid-December. Even here in Jaffa, on the coast of Palestine, the winters were cold.

Still smiling, she pulled her shawl around her shoulders. This journey to Jerusalem was the most cherished Christmas gift she had ever been given. She knew all the great cities of Europe, but she had never come further east. Was it her imagination that this land was so very different from the places she knew? How much is any place seen through the lens of one's imagination, coloured by the dreams one has of it, and of the events that have happened there?

In Paris, does one hear the laughter and music, and see the ghosts of the Revolution and the High Terror? In Rome, does the tramp of the legions sound on the stones? Does one see Caesar with the laurels on his brow, and the world at his feet?

Who does one see in this land, holy to Muslim, Jew and Christian alike?

She should close the window and come in, keep the room warm. And yet she wanted to watch the sky darken until there was only the blaze of stars to see.

Vespasia had known Victor Narraway for many years in connection with Thomas Pitt and the cases he had solved, and in which they had assisted one way or another, but in spite of her silver hair and the refinement of many years in her face, this year of 1900 was only the second of their marriage. Narraway's gift of a journey to Jerusalem had surprised her. There was a spiritual resonance to it she would not have expected from him. She knew his ethical beliefs very well. She could not have married a man whose driving forces she did not know, but he had never framed them in terms of religion. But then perhaps she had not either. One could kneel in church among scores of people who used the same words as you did, many long familiar, and yet the meanings they each took from them were probably worlds apart.

There was so much to discover, even in those you knew best. She hoped it would always be so. One should be growing, changing, learning for ever. Ideas in the mind were like the blood in the veins. The heart that does not beat is dying.

She heard movement behind her and turned.

Narraway was standing in the middle of the room, smiling. In the soft candlelight he looked very dark, and the usual lines of anxiety were eased away, as if he had left all responsibilities behind.

'You'll get cold,' he warned her.

'Yes, I know,' she admitted. 'I was waiting for the stars.' She pulled the windows closed and fastened the lock. 'It's too early for dinner. If I take a cloak, we could go for a walk. Perhaps towards the sea? It's only half a mile or so.'

'No,' he said a trifle too quickly. 'It would be unwise to walk in the streets after dark.' A flicker of concern crossed his face. 'In fact, it might be better not to go towards the dockside even in daylight.'

'I know there's unrest,' she replied. 'But isn't that a little . . .?'

'No, it isn't,' he answered, his face sombre. 'There's always unease in Palestine, but this time of the year it's worse. Thousands of Christian pilgrims come here on their way to Jerusalem, or Bethlehem. Jews come to the Western Wall, and Muslims to the Dome of the Rock. Feelings are high.' He gave a slight shrug, just the lifting of one shoulder. 'God knows, too often we have little respect for each other's religions or customs, especially if they conflict with our own, and we don't understand them. We don't even try to.'

She heard the sharpness in his voice, and might have mistaken it for temper had she not known the depth of his knowledge. In all the experiences they had shared, very often in connection with matters of importance and danger, she had never seen his nerve fail him. Once he had been Head of Special Branch, that arm of the police service responsible for the detection of treason and threats to the safety of the state from within, as opposed to those who defend from armed attack by other nations. In all her long and frequently interesting life, Vespasia had never known anyone less likely to fear unreasonably.

4

He offered her his arm. 'We'll walk in the garden. It's small, but it's very pleasant, even at this time of the year.'

At the door, he put her cloak around her and she felt his touch linger a moment longer than necessary. It was light, but she was aware of its warmth, and it pleased her.

The garden was indeed small, little more than a wide open courtyard with a few vines on the supporting pillars of the extended roof. A couple of cypress trees rose like black flames beside the fountain, which trickled with slight sound into the stone pool. The four hanging lanterns were too dim to detract from the blaze of stars across the open centre.

'There's hardly room to walk,' he said with regret. 'But at least there's no one here to disturb.' The moment he had said it, she saw that he was mistaken. A shadow detached itself from one of the further pillars, was visible for a moment, then melted into the hollow of the arcade and disappeared. She felt his hand tighten on her arm and she stopped.

'Possibly a servant,' she said quietly. It was ridiculous to be distressed by it.

'Or someone keeping an assignation,' Narraway suggested, beginning to move again.

Vespasia looked upward at the sweep of stars, now that the darker sky made them brilliant. 'I imagine they'll be even better out in the desert, when we take the train to Jerusalem. The stars seem so much further away in London; here they look almost close enough to touch – just stretch a little more, stand on tiptoe. I wonder if that is why Christ was born in a place like this.'

'For the stars?' he said with disbelief.

'Well, Wise Men could hardly follow the star on a winter night in London,' she said reasonably.

'Do you believe that, about the star?' he asked with interest, and perhaps a shadow of amusement. He was standing a little behind her, close enough to keep the faint breeze from chilling her. 'If they could see it, why couldn't everyone else? Why couldn't Herod, for a start? Didn't he ask them where it led, and to come back and tell him?'

She was silent for a moment. She had not considered it before. Indeed, why had the frightened, jealous Herod not seen the star himself? Why did he need the Wise Men to return and tell him where it had guided them?

'I don't know,' she said at last. 'Perhaps you only recognise what you are looking for.'

'But he was looking for it,' Narraway pointed out.

She thought for a moment longer. 'He was looking for a rival king, in order to kill him while he was still an infant. The Wise Men were looking for a different kind of king, one to whom they brought gifts, symbolic of who he was.'

'Really?' His voice lifted with mild curiosity.

'Gold for the king, frankincense for the priest and myrrh for the sacrifice,' she told him.

'I didn't know that was what they meant,' he admitted. 'Do you want to walk out into the next courtyard? It goes beyond the archway there.'

'What a good idea,' she agreed. 'Then in to dinner.'

They were still early for the meal, and found themselves in a very pleasant lounge where they asked if they might join an elderly man who was sitting alone near the fire. His hair was white, and his high-browed aquiline face was weathered by wind and sun, and – Vespasia guessed – by much thought. The lines in it were etched deeply, and yet they only added to the beauty of his repose.

Narraway introduced himself and Vespasia, and

they took the offered seats near him. The man spoke of his occupation as an astronomer, but he did not offer them his name.

'You are English,' he said with a smile. 'Much travelled, perhaps, but I think this is your first time in this land, whatever name you choose to give it.'

'Yes,' Narraway agreed. 'And you?'

The man smiled. 'I confess, I travel so much I sometimes forget where I began. The world is full of interest, and beauty. The span of one life offers barely a taste of it: just sufficient to know that it is infinitely precious. Are you perhaps journeying to Jerusalem for Christmas?' His eyes were bright and he regarded them carefully. 'And yet you do not look like pilgrims, in the ordinary sense.' He smiled, to rob his words of presumption. There was great gentleness in his face, and also perhaps a shadow, as if he saw, even at this moment, some of the darker things one does not easily mention to strangers.

'Our visit is a Christmas gift,' Vespasia told him. 'Do you know the country well?'

'Very,' the man replied. 'I shall go to Jerusalem again this year, for Christmas.' He hesitated. 'I think.' The shadow was in his eyes again, and he looked for a moment beyond Vespasia, as if someone had pushed the door to the lounge open but gone away again without coming in.

'You go often?' she asked.

The man smiled as if filled with many memories. It was a sweet expression. 'Very,' he replied. 'But whilst you are here, there are other cities you must see as well. Petra, for example. You approach it on horseback, through a great defile in the cliffs, and suddenly there it is in front of you, rose red, as if it were not man-made, but has grown up out of the rich, burning rock round it.'

He was travelling in a vision of his own, and neither Vespasia nor Narraway interrupted him.

'Or Persepolis,' he went on. 'You stand there in the evening light, like this, as if you were a traveller in time. The ruins of empires tower slender and exquisite into the sky, and you hear the camel bells as the caravans pass, eternal journeymen through time, exactly as they were a thousand years ago, or two thousand, or five. Abraham could have paid his tithes to Melchizedek, and fled on his way into Egypt just so.' He looked at Narraway. 'To step aside from the forward flow of time every now and again is a good thing. As long, of course, as you do not forget

9

to return to the present. There is much to do, battles to be fought, wounds to heal. But from the look in your eyes, perhaps you know that?'

Narraway smiled back at him. 'Not in what remains of this year. We are on holiday. It is the first real one we have had together. Events have always intruded before. Perhaps we stayed too close to home.' There was a touch of regret in his voice, and Vespasia heard it. She would have reached out to touch him, had they been alone.

The old man's face was wistful. 'My dear friend, Jerusalem is the heart's home to all of us, and there is no escaping it.'

Once again Vespasia, facing the doorway more than the others, was aware of a shadow beyond. The moment was so small it could almost have been an illusion, except for the breath of coldness it sent through her. They were being watched by someone who did not wish it to be known.

She forced it from her mind and joined in the conversation about travel until they were called to dinner. As if it were a tacit understanding, she invited the old man to join them, and he accepted with evident pleasure.

The food was simple but delicious, a delicately

flavoured white fish, with only the lightest sauce, and a grain she had not tasted before, flavoured with herbs. There was also a light dessert, a delicate pastry filled with fresh fruit. However, the chief pleasure was the conversation. They spoke of cities and of people. The old man had visited places that neither Vespasia nor Narraway had seen. He described Isfahan.

'I remember standing on the cool sand in the night,' he said quietly. 'The ancient minarets towered up into a sky almost white with stars, and there was not even a whisper of the wind. Then I heard the camels, and they appeared out of the darkness, piled high with who knows what? Silks, spices, ivory, gold. They came towards me with that strange, lurching gait that they have, at once so awkward, and yet so graceful, and there was no sound in the night except the bells. I thought of the old silk road, of Samarkand, and also Trebizond, and other places with marvellous names.'

Narraway spoke a little of Bruges, and St Petersburg, and other cities built upon canals. But even more they spoke of ideas. Some things were remembered with laughter, some with sadness, all were unique.

'Such dreams,' the old man said gently. 'As if we could climb high enough to reach the stars in heaven.'

Again Vespasia saw, in the corner of her vision, the shadow pass the doorway and disappear again. It was without the shading of fabric or the form of a man, the catching of the light on a shoulder or the curve of a head or face.

'Someone is watching us,' she said in a low voice, leaning closer to the old gentleman, thinking he might know who it was. Then, instantly, she thought how foolish it sounded.

'I know,' the old man agreed quietly with a sudden bleakness in his face. 'I think the time is close. Perhaps tonight, or tomorrow.' He looked up to address them both. 'Share this bottle of wine with me, in the name of companionship.'

Vespasia felt a coldness like a fourth presence in the room. She looked at Narraway, but there was nothing in his face to suggest that he had felt it too or that he had heard their brief exchange. She accepted the wine, blood red in the lamplight, and drank to companionship in the journey, and wondered if each of them meant something different by the words. She had thought of the warmth, the love of discovery, friendship, however brief. Did the old man

12

mean something more? She glanced at Narraway, but saw only interest in his face.

The next day was fine and the wind off the sea had less of a bitter edge to it. Vespasia and Narraway made use of the opportunity to explore the city and learn a little of its history. It was a pleasure because it did not matter if they recalled anything but the delight of it, the colour and the variety. They hurried in nothing, fell into conversation with other travellers, but more often with the residents whose ancestors had traded across the Mediterranean since biblical times, and seen the great empires of the past come and go around these shores. Narraway warned her that some of the stories were no more than legend.

'Some legends are a greater truth,' she answered him.

He laughed. 'What on earth do you mean by that?'

The answer was ready on her tongue. 'A general truth rather than a particular one,' she said with a smile. 'Does it matter?'

'Not in the slightest,' he agreed. They were walking easily, casually. For the only time that she could remember, he had no responsibilities. She was observing an easier, softer side of him than she had seen before. He laughed more often. He concentrated on the moment, and with a pleasure in details. He enjoyed conversations, and was even willing to bargain in the market for a small carving of a dog. He paid more for it than it was worth, but he had haggled the price for fun, not to save money.

Vespasia thought of the watcher from the shadows the night before, and wondered now if it had been her imagination. Perhaps he was merely a messenger of some sort, perhaps looking for a particular person to give a letter or message, and unwilling to interrupt other guests.

They bought lunch from a stall and ate it standing in the sun and the wind, watching ships coming and going. They met another English couple, resident in Jaffa, with whom, it transpired in conversation, they had many acquaintances in common, and accepted their invitation to dinner. Their home was that mixture of familiar and alien that inveterate travellers create. There were pictures of the Queen on the wall, books of Kipling's poetry on the shelves, and paintings of English landscapes above Turkish brass ornaments, and exquisite Persian miniatures painted on bone.

Over an excellent meal, they discussed the shaky

political situation in the Middle East in general and this part of it in particular.

'Something of a cauldron,' their host said grimly. His name was Bailey. 'Comes to the boil every so often. Ruled by the Turks, of course. But they don't call Turkey "the sick man of Europe" for no reason.' They were drinking coffee and he passed a dish of cashew nuts across the table. 'The Jews want a homeland, and you can't blame them for that, poor devils! Christians think the shrines, at least, belong to them,' he went on. 'Still feel the kind of daft entitlement that the Crusaders did.' He glanced at Vespasia. 'Sorry if I tread on your religious feelings, Lady Narraway. Been guilty of that rather too often, I'm afraid. You're not on a pilgrimage, are you?'

She smiled at him. She was not fond of religious extremists and never had been. 'I think pilgrimage is an internal journey, more than a matter of where you are geographically,' she replied, taking one of the cashews. 'And if you offend others, or claim ownership of something highly disputed, by right of inheritance or force of arms, I believe you have defeated any spiritual purpose you might originally have had.'

There was a minute's silence, then considered

agreement, which perhaps was in part just out of good manners.

They pursued the subject of the volatile situation in the Holy Land, and Vespasia was keen to listen more than she spoke. She began to appreciate more of the passions behind the current turmoil. She was aware of the fading power of the Ottoman Empire ruled by Turkey, the Arabic-speaking world, Egypt and the ancient cultures of Persia, and the vast hinterland stretching all the way to the borders of Russia and India. They were far larger and more complex than she, as a Western European, had real-ised, and older than England's mere two thousand years. What interested her were the problems right here, and what might concern the people around her.

'Are they afraid of a change of rule?' she asked. 'What would that mean for them?'

'I think to many it is the threat of slow collapse,' their host replied. 'Like everyone else, they dislike the unknown. And unfortunately when an old power fears that it is about to be overthrown, it becomes even more restrictive, overbearing, seeks to collect even higher taxes. To say nothing of the religious turmoil caused by one city being the heart and core of three great faiths.' He went on to describe a few incidents so that they might better understand.

It was past midnight when Vespasia and Narraway left the Baileys' house, and they were grateful to have a servant escort them the mile or so back to the hotel. It was an agreeable walk, sufficient to get a breath of night air after sitting so long in a warm room, but not so much as to be tiring. However, without the servant accompanying them, they might well have missed a turning and become lost, maybe have been robbed. It was a distance Vespasia would not have walked alone at this hour, even in London.

They thanked him when they reached the hotel and went inside with a feeling of relief. At the top of the stairs they passed what they knew to be the old man's room. It was approaching one o'clock in the morning, and yet when Vespasia glanced at the door, she noticed it was not quite closed.

'Do you think he means it to be like that?' she asked with a moment of anxiety. 'Anyone might go in.'

Narraway looked at it, and then bent forward. Without touching the handle, he nudged it gently with the back of his hand. It swung wider, soundlessly.

Vespasia heard his very softly indrawn breath.

'What is it?' she whispered.

He turned and grasped her arm. 'No!'

'What is it? she whispered again, wondering why his fingers dug into her. Did he really imagine she would intrude into the old man's privacy?

'Wait,' he ordered. He let go of her and, placing himself between her and the room, pushed the door open further and stepped forward, blocking her view.

She was mildly irritated. Surely he knew she had some sense of propriety?

Then she heard him give a little sigh and move back towards her. In the light from the passageway she was alarmed at the shock that was in his eyes.

'What is it, Victor?'

'He's dead,' he said very quietly. 'No! You can't go in there.' He barred the doorway with his body. 'His throat has been cut and his room ransacked. From the mess it looks as if his assailant was searching for something.' The anger drained out of his voice. 'You should go to our room. I'll go down and inform the hall porter. It is very obviously murder. He will have to call the police, whatever force deals with such things.' He reached into his pocket and passed her the key. 'Lock the door as soon as you are inside,' he added.

'No, thank you,' she declined. 'I have no reason to suppose that the lock on our door is any better than the lock on his. And we might be supposed to have more that is worth stealing than he did.' Even as she said the words, she expected his contradiction. She was clinging on for a few moments longer to what she wished to be true.

Narraway did not argue. The anger and sorrow left his face and there was only gentleness left. 'My dear, his throat was cut. I don't think this was simply a hotel room robbery. Whatever his murderers were looking for, it was not jewellery or money. The whole room has been torn apart. And if they wished to keep him silent while they stole, why go to such extremes? For what? The money an old man carries when he takes a train journey of a mere six hours?'

'What do you think he had?' she asked. She found herself fighting tears for an old man who had seemed nothing but wise and gentle, an explorer who loved the beauty of the world.

'I don't know.' He stopped evading the issue. 'Knowledge, I should think, but of what, I don't know. Some uprising, perhaps, or even an archaeological find. The land is one of the richest on earth in its past. And the most likely to be controversial. That seems the most likely reason for silencing him.'

'Victor, what have we stumbled into?'

'I've no idea. If it's political, it's very ugly. But the Middle East is not my area of expertise.' He pulled the door closed behind him, but the catch was broken and it did not fasten.

'Political? If it is religious then it is a great deal uglier! How can one murder and ransack the room of an old man, in the name of any God?' Vespasia asked.

'Men have burned others alive, and broken the bodies of women on the wheel in the name of Christ. What is it you think they couldn't do?' His voice caught in his throat with the emotion of it. 'Come.' He took her arm again. 'We must go and tell the poor man on the desk in the lobby that he has a murder on his hands.'

She gave him back the key, and they walked together back down the way they had come, finding the porter at the bottom of the stairs.

'Is something wrong, sir?' the man said politely.

20

Narraway did not hesitate. He spoke quietly. 'On our way we passed the bedroom of the elderly man with whom we dined last night. It was open. I'm afraid he has been robbed, and appears to have been killed. I'm sorry, but it is extremely unpleasant and you will need to see that no one else enters the room before the authorities arrive.'

The man suddenly turned pale. Vespasia was alarmed that he might pass out and be of no use to the situation at all.

'Pull yourself together,' she said quite gently. 'You are in charge, and must take control. Find a messenger and send him straight away to whatever authority is in charge of dealing with crimes. You had better write a note, explaining the urgency of the matter. And put someone to stand guard at the poor man's door. You want this tragedy to be dealt with as quietly and as discreetly as possible.'

The man was shaken to the core. 'I'm only the night porter!' he protested. 'I can't—'

'You are the man in charge,' Narraway said briskly. 'I will remain here at the desk while you go and waken at least two of your staff, preferably three. Quickly!'

The man obeyed with alacrity.

Half an hour later it was all accomplished. The dreadful bedroom was temporarily locked and sealed. The hall porter had found some reserve of courage and had taken control of the situation regarding the guests. The police had been sent for and arrived, led by a very dark-faced, rather handsome man who spoke Arabic, English and French with ease.

After looking at the bedroom, and the body, he returned and asked Vespasia if she was well enough to be questioned.

'Certainly,' she replied with a touch of asperity. 'I am grieved. He seemed a particularly wise and gentle man, but I had not known him before yesterday evening. I am not incapacitated.'

A flicker of amusement crossed his face, and vanished. 'Thank you, Mrs Narraway,' he said quietly. 'I am obliged to you.'

She did not correct him.

Narraway did. 'Lady Narraway,' he said softly.

The policeman's eyebrows rose.

'I am Lord Narraway,' Narraway continued. 'I was Head of Special Branch in England. Now I sit in the House of Lords, and consult occasionally on certain matters to do with treason, civil unrest and so on. We did not mention it earlier because we are on holiday, and it was irrelevant.'

The policeman thought for a moment before replying. His face was as bland as he could make it. His difficulty was clear.

Narraway gave a slight smile. 'We have passports, naturally. I would consider you less than competent if you did not wish to see them.'

The man relaxed. 'Thank you, sir.' He glanced in the direction of the tragic room with its blood-soaked corpse. 'Have you any idea what happened, sir?'

'No,' Narraway admitted. 'We spent this evening with a Mr and Mrs Bailey in their home. We had dinner and an excellent historical and philosophical conversation. The evening before, we dined here with this gentleman, but I regret now that I did not even ask his name. I know only that he intended travelling to Jerusalem and expressed some urgency about being there before Christmas Day.'

'Did he say why?'

'No. In fact he was very discreet about it altogether.'

'Whoever killed him looks to have searched the room thoroughly and violently. Did he mention that he was carrying anything of value enough to cause such a thing?'

A half-memory flickered through Vespasia's mind, but before she could clarify it, Narraway answered.

'Nothing. He appeared to travel abstemiously . . . I mean with little . . .'

The policeman made a bleak little gesture with his hand. 'I know the word, sir.' He shrugged. 'There is nothing to suggest he was a rich man. He carried only necessities for travel, cleanliness and prayer, as far as we can see.'

'Perhaps whoever killed him succeeded in finding whatever it was, and took it?' Narraway suggested.

The man looked doubtful. 'Perhaps . . .'

Narraway moved a step closer to Vespasia and touched her arm lightly. 'Then if we can be of no further help, we will retire. We plan to leave on the two o'clock train for Jerusalem. I hope that does not hamper your investigation?' It was as close as he intended to come to asking permission to leave.

'I have no reason to detain you,' the policeman agreed. 'My man here will follow you upstairs and perhaps you will be good enough to show him your passports? So I may say I was diligent, you understand?'

'Of course,' Narraway agreed.

'I regret that your stay in our country has been marred by such an unpleasant event.' He glanced at Vespasia for only the second time. 'My lady . . .' He cleared his throat. 'I imagine you have no observation you can add?' It was an acknowledgement of her presence, a courtesy rather than a question.

Vespasia was slightly stung by his assumption; then she dismissed it as childish, a rather emotional reaction because she was deeply grieved.

'Actually I have,' she answered, meeting his eyes, 'although I am not sure if it is of any use to you. He appeared at dinner to be a little nervous. Three times at least, I observed someone watching him from beyond the archway that led out of the dining room. It was very quick, and in the shadows, but he seemed disturbed by it.'

Narraway looked at her with surprise.

The policeman frowned. 'And you did not mention this to your husband?' There was disapproval in his voice.

She met his eye without a flicker. 'Had I known it was more than a mere nuisance, I would have, but as it was, we had other things to discuss at the time. I am still not certain it was more than my imagination.' As she said it, she realised that she was certain that

that was a lie. She was not a nervous woman. She had travelled all over Europe, facing discomfort and even danger with equanimity. She had never fainted in her life, and she had spoken as an equal to half the princes, prelates and political leaders in the world. Yet she knew both danger and evil, and the watcher in the shadows beyond the doorway troubled her.

'Of course, my lady.' The policeman bowed. 'I did not mean to be discourteous. Thank you for bringing it to my attention.'

He did not believe her. She had half expected it. She smiled at him, not envying his task, and accepted Narraway's arm to leave and go up to their room.

As soon as the door was closed and Narraway had wedged a chair against it also, should the lock not hold, he turned to her.

'Why did you not tell me that someone was watching the old man?' His voice was quite soft, but it demanded an answer.

'Because it was only a shadow, and I knew he was already aware of it,' she answered. 'There was nothing to say, and our thoughts were, by then, elsewhere.'

A very faint colour warmed his cheeks, and she wondered if it embarrassed him.

'Perhaps I should have,' she said meekly. 'But it didn't seem to matter. Would it have made a difference?'

He shook his head minutely. 'I doubt it. Poor man.' He turned away and took his jacket off, ready to hang it up, then felt something in his pocket. He took it out slowly. It was the thinnest possible piece of parchment, irregularly shaped, as if it had been torn from a larger piece. He opened it carefully. There was a far smaller piece of ordinary paper inside it.

'What is it?' she asked.

'I don't know.' He raised his head from staring at it and his expression was one of total puzzlement. 'I haven't seen it before.'

'But it was in your pocket!'

He looked back at it. The smaller piece had writing on it, in English. He read it aloud.

The Watcher draws near, and I am afraid I will not be able to deliver this myself. I entrust it to you, for the sake of all mankind. Take it to the House of Bread on the Via Dolorosa. It must be there by Christmas Eve. May the hand of God protect you.

There was no signature.

They stared at each other for several moments.

Vespasia's mind raced through possibilities. Did he suspect his death? Or only fear it as a matter of precaution? What could possibly be for the sake of all mankind? Was that an exaggeration, to make them more likely to pick up his cause? Or did he believe it? She was loath to think him deceptive. Could she really be so mistaken in her judgement of him? Why was it so urgent? To do with some political uprising? Regardless, to play the coward now would be to deny everything she had lived for all her long and adventure-filled years. In her youth she had stood with musket in hand at the barricades of revolution in Rome. In her maturity, she had fought in politics and in espionage with words. She had given considerable money to causes she believed in and risked her reputation to support them.

'Vespasia—' Narraway began.

'We must do it,' she cut across him. 'And to be purely practical, my dear, if you try to go alone, how long do you think it will be before someone has the idea to hold me hostage against your returning this piece of parchment to them? If it is really so important, they would be stupid not to.'

Narraway had never wasted time in pointless argument, and he did not do so now. He spread the parchment out and looked at it closely. It was covered in writing he could not read. He was not sure even what language it was. The letters were uneven, as if written under the stress of great emotion, and it was signed at the end with a single name.

He turned to Vespasia, puzzled.

She studied it also, then looked at him curiously, wondering if he were as inexplicably moved by it as she was. The edge was nearly straight above where the writing began, as if this were the end of a longer piece. She had no idea what it said, and yet the passion in it seemed to cling to the parchment even after centuries. 'We must take it,' she said quietly. 'He gave it to you, expecting his own death. It is a trust we must honour.'

He refolded the parchment, following exactly the folds that had been in it before. Then he put it in the small, satin pocket of the lining of his jacket.

'We had better pack early and leave the hotel. We must be sure to catch our train. We have only one day if we are to make the deadline,' he said. 'And get some sleep now.' He looked at the alarm clock on the bedside table. 'It's twenty minutes to three. We'll have perhaps four or five hours' rest.' He looked grave, still worried.

She was a little older than he, a fact she wished to ignore, if possible even forget. She knew precisely what was in his mind.

'If you ask me if I am all right,' she warned him, 'I shall not forgive you easily. I am sure you do not wish that!' She smiled, because it was not really out of anger that she spoke, but the self-consciousness of a very beautiful woman who was nevertheless aware that time was leaving its mark on her. Her face would always be beautiful: the sweep of her brow, the high cheekbones, the curve of her jaw and neck, the way she held her head. But she had lived long and passionately, and it was written in her countenance.

She walked like a queen, but not quite so quickly. The fierce energy of her mind was not diminished, but now and then her body let her down.

He was smiling back at her. He had no intention of repeating past slips of the tongue. He was vulnerable too, in entirely different ways, but he understood the pain, even if for him it was different.

'I think we should be at the station by one o'clock,'

he answered, as if all other matters had been settled, as indeed they had.

Vespasia did not sleep well. Her dreams were haunted by the gentle face of the old man who had been so violently murdered not forty feet away, and under the same roof. He must have known that the Watcher was coming for him when they had said good night after that lovely dinner over which they had discussed so much. That was the last opportunity he had had to slip the paper into Narraway's pocket. And yet he had parted from them with such grace, as if they would meet again the next day, and nothing terrible would happen.

For a moment she had been a trifle annoyed that Narraway had so instinctively stepped across the doorway so she did not see inside the room and catch a glimpse of the dead man with his throat slashed. Now that they were married, he protected her often, as if it were his duty, or his privilege to guard her from unpleasantness. He had never done so before. For most of their long acquaintance, he had been Mr Narraway, Head of Special Branch: clever, often ruthless and very much alone. She had been Lady Vespasia Cumming-Gould, daughter of an earl and possibly the most beautiful woman of her generation. He would not have taken the liberty! If he had dared, she would have raised an eyebrow, and he would have retreated and apologised, albeit with amusement. They had become friends at first, then been thoroughly taken aback to find they wished deeply to be more than that, very much more. But he really would have to stop treating her as if she were fragile! She had a will as strong as Toledo steel! Or perhaps she should come closer to home: as Sheffield steel?

And yet the thought of the gentle old man so brutally murdered shocked her.

'Victor,' she said quietly when they were at breakfast.

He had been deep in thought. He looked up. 'Yes?'

'I dreamed about the old man most of the night. I'm glad you did not let me see him. I liked him very much.'

'I, too,' he said quietly. 'I wish he had had time to tell us a little more. I couldn't make any sense out of the paper. There is no picture, no writing legible to us, and not enough of anything even to make out if it is part of a map.'

'Presumably the person we take it to will know,' she suggested.

'I hope so.' He looked beyond her through the archway towards the entrance hall. 'There seem to be police all over the place today. I suppose it's inevitable. I haven't seen the French couple who sat by the window. I imagine they've found other accommodation. I'd have booked us a seat on another train if I could have, but I know there isn't one.'

'There isn't?'

'Just one train,' he replied. 'Leaves Jerusalem in the morning, gets here in the middle of the day, and goes back in the afternoon. Something to do with the track.'

She was puzzled. 'I thought you said the railway was British? Why on earth did we do that?'

'It is,' he agreed with a flicker of amusement. 'And I've no idea why. Most things come down to money in the end. Would you prefer to leave the hotel and have an early lunch somewhere in the town?'

She considered. She would far rather not stay here, but she also did not wish to sit in a café with a pile of suitcases, and rely on the erratic public transport to get them to the station on time. They must be in Jerusalem to deliver the curious piece of paper no later than Christmas Eve.

'No, thank you.' It was the only possible decision.

'And if we stay here in the hotel there is the very small chance that we may learn something of use, such as who may have killed the old man. I dislike it very much that I do not even know his name! It seems so . . . heartless.'

He smiled at her across the table. 'Then we shall have to give him a name. How about Balthazar?'

She was momentarily puzzled.

'Did you not listen to him?' He raised his dark brows. 'He was very wise . . .'

She smiled and for a moment tears stung her eyes. 'Of course. He was a wise man journeying to Jerusalem, with a gift, to be there in time for Christmas. Balthazar was the third named, at least in legend. Presumably he carried the myrrh, symbolising sacrifice.' The tears now slid down her cheeks and she felt oddly vulnerable because of it. She was justifying every thought he might have that she was weaker than he. 'It seems horribly appropriate.' She took a shaky breath, struggling to control herself. This fear was ridiculous, but as real as the hard wooden table in front of her, or the stone tiles of the floor. 'What have we got ourselves into, Victor?'

'Jerusalem.' He hesitated only an instant, glanced

at her hand on the white tablecloth, then deliberately did not move to touch her. 'City of promise, glory and sacrifice – from Isaac to Christ, and only God knows how many others. This is your last chance to change your mind. We could find a ship home again, or to Alexandria, Rome, even Constantinople, which used to be Byzantium. I believe it is one of the most complex and most fascinating cities in the world.'

'Yes.' She heard her own voice as if it were that of a stranger. 'I've heard so too. But I am going to Jerusalem.'

'I know that, but I had to ask.'

She did not look at him, in case emotion overtook her again. In the short space they had been together, less than two years, she had been happier than at any other time in her life. Every day was infinitely precious. Why should she take unknown risks to deliver a meaningless piece of paper for a stranger who would never know whether she did it or not?

She knew the answer. Because to be alive is risk; to care is to be vulnerable. The only safety there is lies in doing your best, being the bravest and most generous you can.

She ate a piece of toast, which was strange and flat, not in the least like English bread, and finished her tea, not really tasting any of it.

They remained in the hotel lounge all morning, apart from the brief time it took to pack their cases including a picnic for the journey, which Vespasia ordered from the hotel kitchen. But, waiting there, they did not learn anything of interest, or observe more than the local police continuing to question various staff, and making searches that did not appear to yield any helpful results.

They left a little after noon, and travelled towards the railway station in a fairly comfortable brougham drawn by a single horse. The journey was without incident until two blocks short of the station when the driver made a sharp turn to the right and then another, away from the station altogether.

Narraway leaned forward to speak to the driver to attract his attention. 'Railway station, please!' he said distinctly. Then when the man took no notice, he repeated it, first in French, then in German. The man did not even turn in his seat. Instead, he pulled the horse to a halt.

Vespasia felt a chill of fear. A man in a dark robe

was walking along the pavement to the right of them. He would be level with them in a dozen strides.

She looked to the left, and saw a tall, thin man walking, holding a long stick, like a shepherd's crook, the curved end of it level with his head. It was stout enough to lean on, and would make an excellent weapon.

Suddenly she was deeply afraid. What could she use to defend herself? She looked around, but there was nothing. She was aware of Narraway, rigid beside her. She knew perfectly well that he had no weapon either. Were the men now so close ordinary robbers, looking to take their luggage, and any money they might have? Or were they somehow aware of Balthazar's paper, and that was what they wanted?

The luggage she did not care about. There was nothing in it she could not replace. The man with the staff drew level with her and moved off the side of the road to the centre, shifting the staff to hold it as a weapon. Vespasia picked up the smallest piece of baggage, an attaché case with soft sides and hard corners.

The man to the right also moved into the road, coming closer.

Narraway shot to his feet and lunged forward, seizing the driver, who was sitting motionless, and toppling him off his seat sideways, hard so that he fell to the ground. His weight knocked over the man in the street and sent both sprawling.

Vespasia struck out as hard as she could with the attaché case, the reinforced corners of it hitting the man on the side of his face. He lurched sideways, putting his hands over his eyes, temporarily blinding himself.

Narraway grasped the reins, shouting as loudly as he could, startling the horse and urging it forward. The animal obeyed, and the carriage wheels struck and then bounced over the men trying to get up from the road. One screamed in pain.

Vespasia sat down very hard, sideways across the seat, still clutching the case.

The carriage picked up speed, and another carriage came out of an alley ahead of them. There was a man driving it, and two startled women in the seats.

Vespasia righted herself with difficulty as they swept past the women and round the corner into the traffic again.

They reached the railway station and drew up at the side of the road.

A porter appeared to assist with luggage. Narraway somewhat awkwardly climbed down and offered his hand to Vespasia.

'Are you all right?' he asked with concern, searching her face to read in it how badly shaken she was.

'Perfectly, thank you,' she assured him with as much dignity as she could muster. 'What are you going to do with the horse?'

'Nothing,' he answered without hesitation. 'It's a good enough animal. Someone will be glad to care for it. We should get off the street as quickly as possible.' He kept his hand on her arm. 'It's still half an hour before the train leaves, but if it arrived on time we should be able to take our seats. We need to be in a crowd.' He looked at her again, more closely, the anxiety clear in his eyes.

'I'm a little dusty, that's all,' she answered his clear concern. 'And it seems to me that everyone else is either dusty, or muddy. It seems to have rained.'

He gave a quick bark of laughter, then became sober again. 'How very English to consider the weather, my dear. Let us go into the station. I still have the tickets, fortunately.'

She hesitated only a moment. 'Do you still have Balthazar's letter?'

There was surprise and disbelief in his face. 'Do you think it was because of that?'

He was right. It was absurd. Who would know about it anyway?

'No,' she agreed. 'No, of course not. Nevertheless, do you still have it? We must deliver it if we can, for Balthazar's sake.'

He put his hand into his inside pocket. 'Yes. I have it.' He looked uncomfortable.

'What is it?' she asked.

They walked through the graceful arches into the station building, on the heels of the porter. There were already considerable numbers of people milling around, calling out to each other, and of course the usual pedlars offering any number of useful or edible things for sale: sweetmeats, matches, bootlaces, almonds and pecans, dried fruit.

He stood close to her, one arm around her shoulders, lightly, but she was very aware of it. It was comfortable, and at the moment she was unusually glad of it.

'I think it is time we faced the truth,' she said, staring straight ahead of her. 'He was murdered for something, Victor, and I don't think it was money. Anyone looking at him would doubt he had much. We would be far more likely to have something to justify the risk of an ordinary robbery.'

'You are right,' he agreed, deep reluctance in his voice. 'And I suppose we have been given the trust to take the parchment to the bakery, or whatever it is, in Jerusalem. And at Christmas! Not a good time to break your word.' He said it lightly, but when she looked at his face it was unusually grave. He did not meet her eyes, as if his own seriousness embarrassed him slightly.

'Actually, it is not necessarily a bakery,' she told him. 'He calls it "the House of Bread". Symbolically, bread is life.'

'I wonder if there is only one bakery on the Via Dolorosa,' he thought aloud. 'I suppose a street so old doesn't have numbers.'

'It may not be the original Via Dolorosa,' she answered, watching the crowds pass by them. They were the passengers from Jerusalem arrived on the morning train. 'But it doesn't matter. The actuality is nothing. The meaning is all.'

He was looking away from her, watching everyone that passed by.

He glanced up at the station clock. 'In a few minutes we'll be able to board the train,' he said as the crowds thinned. 'If we are lucky we'll have a first-class coach largely to ourselves.' He gave the porter a couple of coins and motioned him to follow with the luggage.

It was noisy, crowded, and the engine belched steam at irregular intervals, but – like at all railway stations – there was a breath of excitement in the air, the promise of travel, broad landscapes, open spaces, cities new to the mind but old as history itself, and closer to the heart.

When they were settled, they did indeed have considerable space and quite a bit of comfort. They sat next to the window, opposite each other, Vespasia facing forward.

'The original Wise Men came on camels,' Narraway observed with a smile. 'And from the east, I believe.'

'Do you?' she asked, realising with an overwhelming sense of the strangeness of it that she did not really know if he believed anything of the Christmas story. She had thought it mattered, but now the idea occurred to her that perhaps it was the 'star' you were following that eventually dictated where you would arrive.

'That Wise Men riding camels followed a star to

Jerusalem?' he asked. His face was impossible to read. He did not want to hurt her, and he realised he did not know how literally she believed the charm and the symbolism of Christianity. Now that the question was raised, she did not know either. Suddenly it had all become very serious.

'My dear, stars do not sit over a specific place,' he said gently. 'The earth turns, giving us the illusion that the stars move. The Pole Star perhaps is fixed for us, precisely because it is above the Pole, but not the others.'

She considered what he was asking.

'Actually they came to Jerusalem first, where Herod was,' she replied, although of course it was irrelevant, wasn't it? She had not considered before whether the journey was meant to be literal, or merely metaphorical. 'The star was over Bethlehem,' she added.

The train engine belched steam. A whistle shrilled and they lurched forward, stopped, then they began to move slowly, but gathering speed. They were outside the station in the winter sun, passing through the city of Jaffa with its busy streets. In minutes they would be beyond it, pulling away from the coast and inland.

'It doesn't matter where they came from, east or

west,' she continued. 'What matters is that they followed a light, perhaps it was an inner one. And they brought gifts uniquely appropriate.'

'Gold, frankincense, and myrrh,' he agreed. 'You told me their significance, remember?'

She studied his face for a moment, wondering what he believed. It was something they had never discussed. One went to church on Sundays, now and then, and believed most of the morality of the faith. Beyond that, it was among the subjects that it was considered ill-mannered to discuss in any depth. People were easy to offend.

They were passing through farmland now, olive groves and occasionally fields of some grain crop. The earth was dry, but it held its own kind of beauty. Was that because the imagination peopled it with the stories from the Bible?

'And what on earth is it we are bringing?' Narraway asked wryly. 'A piece of paper that seems to make no sense at all!'

'A promise,' Vespasia said without irritation. 'Maybe it will mean something when we get there.'

'To the House of Bread?'

'That's what he said, isn't it?'

'He wrote "House of Bread" in English. But then he would assume we couldn't either speak or read Hebrew,' he pointed out. 'We can enquire.'

'I think the paper would be safer if I carry it,' she said quietly. 'You might have even an inside pocket picked, or take off your jacket for some reason.'

'And where can you carry it?' he asked, his eyebrows raised.

'Oh, Victor, please! Use a little imagination.' She stood up. 'I think I will go along to the cloakroom and place it there now.' She held out her hand.

He was reluctant.

'Please be realistic.' She lowered her voice still further, and smiled ruefully. 'If they are going to tear my clothes off to search me, we are already something of a lost cause.'

'Aren't you placing faith ahead of wisdom?' he asked, all humour vanished.

'With any courage at all, they will do the same thing,' she told him. 'And this is not the time or occasion for a philosophical debate on the end gains of cowardice versus courage, and what one may lose or gain. It would be pointless anyway. We both know that we are going to take this paper to the Bakery!'

'House of Bread,' he corrected her. 'Beit Lechem in Hebrew – or if you prefer – Bethlehem.' He passed her the parchment, folded into a small square and no thicker than two layers of ordinary paper.

She took it with a slightly shaking hand and pushed it into her blouse, just below the neckline. She would conceal it better in the privacy of the toilet at the rear of the coach.

On her return, she was in the corridor keeping her balance with difficulty, when she saw a dark-robed figure come out of a compartment a few yards ahead of her, and start to move forward. His head was bent a little, and he walked with surprising grace, considering the jolt and lurch of the train.

There was something about him that gave her a chill of familiarity. She had seen him before! The black robes had hardly any dust on them, as if he spent his time within houses, never on the street, and he wore boots, coal-black, soft leather boots.

She increased her pace and caught up with him, touching his elbow to draw his attention.

'Excuse me!'

Startled, he turned and looked at her. He had an extraordinary face, with high cheekbones, empty eyes, lips like the slash of a knife. There was no expression in him at all, as if he could not see her, although he must be able to.

The train wheels rattled over the sleepers and seemed to lurch dangerously as they hit a bend. The countryside beyond the windows changed; the distance became blurred.

There were doors at the end of all the carriages, for getting on and off. Vespasia was not far from the one behind her. If she turned away from this man she would pass it, close enough that a quick lunge from him, if the handle turned, and she would be hurled out, as lost as if she were overboard from a ship.

She could not help stepping back, none the less.

He moved forward, his terrible hollow eyes still on hers.

She could not bear the thought of him touching her, and yet if she retreated she was certain she would end back at the door on to the speeding track and death. Did he want the paper? Or only its destruction?

She was still looking into his eyes. 'I beg your pardon.' She found the words difficult to say. 'I thought you were someone I know.'

'I am,' he said. His voice was a whisper, but she

could hear him perfectly, even above the rattle and clank of the train wheels on the rails. 'You have always known me – merely forgotten for a while.'

It was true. She had no doubt whatever that he was the Watcher.

He made an odd little noise in his throat that could have been laughter, then he turned and walked away ahead of her. When he reached her compartment he stopped at the door and put his hand on the latch. He turned it and swung the door open.

She heard Narraway's voice from inside. He started to speak, then ceased, as if the words died in his throat. The Watcher darted down the corridor as another compartment door opened, and then instantly closed again with a slam. Ahead of her a young man stood, owl-faced, staring as if with complete incomprehension.

Vespasia was delighted to see him until she realised that he might quite easily fall victim to the Watcher, who was now nowhere to be seen, as well.

The young man smiled almost absent-mindedly, with a sweet, utterly innocent expression. He took a couple of steps towards them, and as the light from the corridor windows crossed his face, Vespasia could see that he was not so very young. In fact, although his face had no lines in it, no visible mark of time, he was certainly past youth. His features were blunt and quite strong, and completely vacant except for a certain benign hope.

He opened the door to her compartment and then, to her surprise, followed her, closing it when they were both inside.

Narraway rose to his feet. He looked at Vespasia, then at the young man, waiting for an explanation.

Vespasia was still shivering, not with cold but with relief for having escaped what she was certain could have become a violent confrontation. If the Watcher could open the coach doors from the inside, and anyone were pushed out, at speed, it would be almost certain death. She imagined lying there broken boned, dying, with no one but the Watcher even aware that she had gone.

This was ridiculous. The city of Jaffa and the body of Balthazar were behind them. She had merely met the black-robed man in the corridor, a man with empty eyes. He had probably just been taken by surprise.

She made herself smile at Narraway.

'I lost my balance a little in the passageway,' she said simply. 'This gentleman was kind enough to make sure I got back here safely.' She watched the stranger. For the first time she realised he was wearing a Western suit in a sort of pale sand colour, so neutral it was hard to describe.

'Benedict,' he introduced himself. 'The good word.' He smiled slightly. 'A little hard to live up to, but I am full of hope.' He did not say if it was his first or last name.

'Victor Narraway. How do you do?' Narraway replied. 'My wife you have just met.' He looked at Vespasia questioningly, searching to know if she had hidden the paper, and if she was telling the truth about what happened in the corridor.

Yes, she had hidden the paper. But was she telling the truth? She was not certain what the truth was. She would tell him when Benedict excused himself and went back to his own compartment.

Except that he did not. He sat down in the seat next to the door and made himself comfortable. Clearly he intended to stay, uninvited. Vespasia had the darting idea he was a little simple. That look of slight vacancy in his eyes was not a trick of the light, it was really there.

She sat down again in her seat and Narraway sat also.

'I saw someone in the corridor that I think was the same man we saw in the hotel in Jaffa,' she said, hoping he would understand her meaning. 'The man who—'

'I know,' he cut off the rest of her sentence. 'I saw his face when he opened the carriage door. Where is he?'

'He continued down the corridor, but I didn't see where he went . . .'

'He went away.' Benedict looked up with a smile. 'But not far. He is going to Jerusalem also.'

'That's where the train is going,' Narraway said a little tartly.

Vespasia saw a moment's puzzlement in Benedict's face, then the bland sweetness returned.

'He is always going there,' he observed. 'But when he finally arrives, I dare say it will be the end.'

Vespasia had no idea what he meant, if indeed he meant anything at all. She was fast coming to the conclusion that he was simple.

Narraway looked across at him, frowning.

Benedict's smile increased. 'Jerusalem is always the end, isn't it?' he said innocently.

'It's the end of this track,' Narraway agreed. 'At least I think so. But no doubt in the future there'll be tracks all over: to Jericho, Damascus, maybe even further, into Turkey and Egypt and Persia.'

'Of course.' Benedict nodded. 'The whole world will be covered by railway tracks one day. But the last destination will always be Jerusalem.' He was talking complete nonsense as if it were self-evident wisdom.

Vespasia looked across at Narraway to warn him not to argue. Benedict was a nuisance, and she would far rather he got up and left, but he did not look in the least likely to do that. In fact it seemed likely that he would remain for the rest of the six-hour journey.

If the Watcher should return, would they be glad of Benedict's presence, or guilty for the danger in which it would place him? The man appeared too naïve to be aware of anything amiss, even if it hung in the air like a coming storm.

Narraway seemed to have come to the same conclusion. He settled back in his seat without responding, except a slow, careful smile at Vespasia.

'I think on this train we all believe we are going to Jerusalem,' she said mildly.

'Because it says so on the front?' he asked.

'That would be a good reason.' She tried to sound

less impatient than she felt. She really was very far from in a mood to be patient with inane conversation.

'I suppose so,' Benedict conceded. 'But very simple, don't you think? Not everything goes where it says it will, or no one could ever get lost. And we do get lost, you know.'

'You just said a few moments ago that everything goes to Jerusalem,' Narraway pointed out.

'Oh, yes,' Benedict agreed. 'But it isn't always where they thought they were going, is it? And why. What will you find when you get there?' He leaned forward a little. 'What are you looking for?'

'A bakery,' Narraway answered, amusement in his eyes now.

But he had not answered the real question, the one that was now growing stronger in Vespasia's mind. Were they going with a reason of their own, one they knew, or in any deeper way understood?

Benedict nodded. 'Of course. But you surprise me.' He blinked. 'I didn't expect you to know that.'

Vespasia saw a sudden alarm in Narraway's dark face. Had he been foolish to speak the literal and seemingly meaningless truth to this rather irritating man?

'You don't think I know where I'm going?'

Narraway asked. There was no edge of rudeness to his voice, just mild enquiry.

Benedict smiled back with extraordinary sweetness. 'I don't think you have any idea at all,' he replied.

Vespasia wanted to laugh, and yet there was nothing in the least funny in his words. She must be far more distressed by Balthazar's death than she had realised. But of course she was! She had liked the man very much. There was a wisdom and a gentleness in him she could not forget. And she also felt guilty. He had known he was in danger, and she had known it too, and they had done nothing to help him.

And she was also afraid. She had travelled throughout Europe most of her life, but this land was very different from any she knew. In the deepest and most beautiful sense, she was not alone. She loved Narraway more profoundly than she had loved anyone before. They were friends as well as lovers, companions, allies in all quests and battles, as well as the most exquisite pleasures and understandings that had never before been so deep.

All of life was sweeter, and more desperately precious – and brief – than in any time past. There were too few days to treasure, too few to make mistakes or take the future for granted. Pleasure and pain were both so much more intense.

'Do you know where you are going?' she said to Benedict. It was a challenge, and he recognised it.

'Oh, yes,' he said with certainty. 'I do now. But I shall forget, in a while. And then, of course, I may get lost. I hope not.'

Again the answer sounded so straightforward, and was anything but.

'But I shall end in Jerusalem,' he added, seeing her confusion. 'We all will. Including the man in the corridor. But he will not like it.'

'Will we?' she said.

He did not reply for so long that she had decided he did not intend to. Then his face brightened as if he had made a decision. 'Why are you going? Really? Why Jerusalem? Why now?' He spoke as if the answer were of importance to him.

'Because it's Christmas,' Narraway replied. There was still that flash of humour in his eyes.

'Do you believe in Christmas?' Benedict asked perfectly seriously.

Narraway drew in his breath to give an easy answer, and realised that Vespasia was looking at him too.

Was he doing this for her? Or for himself as well? Since Balthazar's murder, it was to keep their promise to him. But before that? Was it a gift, because it was a charming and imaginative thing to do? Or was he going there for himself as well?

She had attended church on and off all her life. Certainly she did not disbelieve in a religion. But that is not the same as believing. It was more a matter of taking a precaution in case it was true. Real believing demands change, loyalty, cost. Sooner or later it would also require sacrifice of some sort, perhaps profound.

Benedict was watching Narraway, waiting. He did not expect to be slighted, made fun of, even gently. He expected a dignified and honest answer. Whether he received one or not was not a test of his sincerity, but a test of Narraway's.

Narraway frowned. 'I'm not sure,' he said at last. 'Perhaps I'm going to find out.'

'Do you want to find out?' Benedict asked, his eyes wide and curious. 'Knowledge is precious, but it's dangerous too. There is a great illusion of freedom in not knowing. There's the illusion of innocence.'

'No, there isn't,' Narraway said immediately. 'Not if it's a choice, and you could have known, if you had wanted to. That's not innocence. It isn't even honesty, it's self-deceit and, at the worst, cowardice.'

'Ah!' Benedict's face lit up with satisfaction, even joy. 'The bittersweet fruit of the tree of know-ledge of good and evil. You would eat, wouldn't you? You would always eat, sooner or later!' He turned to Vespasia. 'And you? Do you believe in Christmas?'

She had a moment of certainty that Benedict was not as innocent as he appeared to be. She would stop gently backing away.

'Whose idea of Christmas?' she challenged him. 'Yours? Mine? The Church's? Popular tradition? Angels singing in the sky? Wise Men bearing gifts, and a star of unique glory that lights the way to salvation – once only?'

Benedict was enjoying himself now, smiling widely. He had beautiful teeth. 'A new star in the sky? I like that, yes! Yes, one by which to navigate the journey of the soul. I like that very much. Is that the Christmas you believe in, lady?'

As she thought about that, the warmth blossomed inside her and opened into a certainty. 'I believe it is. But when the clouds came we lost sight of it. How on earth do sailors navigate in bad weather?'

'Carefully,' Narraway said, only half joking. 'Very carefully.'

She looked at him, wondering now if he dealt only lightly with a subject so intensely serious because he did not want to risk possibly disagreeing with her, even causing a certain disillusion in her; or because perhaps he was not certain if he believed himself. Was he a moralist, but perhaps also an agnostic, and this, of all times, was not the occasion on which to shake her faith?

What did she believe, and possibly more importantly, why? Was it with thought, or only with need? She looked at him again, at his eyes, and she knew only that he would not willingly hurt her.

Benedict was nodding. 'Yes, yes indeed. Very carefully,' he said. 'There is great danger, enemies who are clear, and who know you, at times better than you know yourself. Yes . . . carefully.'

He had barely finished speaking when there was a loud clang from somewhere ahead of them. The train jolted, slid for a few yards along the rails, jolted again more violently, and then stopped altogether.

Vespasia looked out of the window beside her and saw desert: endless rock and sand, bleached of almost all colour. Here and there was the odd twisted, weather-beaten tree. The desert seemed to stretch unbroken to the horizon, without feature, as if there would never be anything else.

Narraway leaned forward and put his hand on hers, gently. He did not say anything. He would not insult her with reassurances that neither of them believed.

She turned to look at Benedict. He was staring through the glass of the carriage door as the man in the dark robes walked by, not looking either to right or left.

'Oh dear,' he said quietly. 'This could become unpleasant. Still, I suppose we were never promised a journey without incident. After all, it is Christmas, and we are going to Jerusalem. We have been waiting a long time.'

'Have we?' Narraway said a little tersely. 'Perhaps you have. We only decided to come a couple of weeks ago.'

Benedict looked at him curiously. 'Really? As recently as that, you think? Still, what is time? Not quite the straight line we imagine. Not that I really know, of course. It seems endless to me.' He looked at the door handle. 'Does this lock, do you suppose?'

Narraway stood up and stepped over to it,

examined it for a moment or two, felt the latch and then turned it with a sharp snap.

'Yes, it does,' he replied, returning to his seat.

'Thank you,' Benedict said with satisfaction. 'We do not wish to have that person in here. I have something I would like to show you. You may find it interesting.'

Outside the sky was getting heavy, dark grey clouds rolling in from the horizon.

'Which way are we going?' Vespasia asked curiously. 'Surely it is early to be getting dark. And night should come in from the east anyway, ahead of us.'

'That's more or less south,' Narraway agreed. 'And yes, it's too early for nightfall, and too quick. It's a storm. They wouldn't stop for a storm, would they? It looks as if it could be snow.' He turned to Benedict.

'It snows here sometimes,' Benedict agreed. 'But very little. And there's little rain either.' He looked less calm than he had done. He was searching his inside pockets for something. After a moment or two he appeared to find it.

There was a rumble of thunder in the distance. Lightning flared across the purple-grey of the clouds and then seconds later there was more thunder.

'Dramatic,' Vespasia said quietly. 'I used to enjoy thunderstorms as a girl, except that the dogs were frightened.'

Benedict pulled a folded piece of paper out of his pocket. With his back to the carriage door, he opened it and spread it out on Vespasia's lap. He said nothing.

She looked at it, expecting a letter of some sort. Then she realised that it was not paper but parchment, not noticeably very different from the piece she had hidden inside her own bodice. It too was covered with script, but different from the one she had. One rough edge of it might match hers, as if they had been torn apart.

Benedict was watching her closely. She would like to have kept her face expressionless, but she knew at least the widening of her eyes would have told him something. He might pretend to be simple, but he was certainly not unobservant.

'Ah . . .' he said again. 'You find it interesting.'

'How did you come by it?' Narraway asked, his voice tight with a tension he could not conceal.

Vespasia knew what was in his mind even before she met his eyes. Had Benedict killed someone to get it? Once he was certain that one of them had Balthazar's paper, would he kill them also and then take it? Was the Watcher his friend, or enemy? Rival or collaborator?

She felt horribly vulnerable.

Outside, the wind stirred up plumes of dust and sand. There was more thunder, and then the rain struck, beating against the windows and sliding down in sheets that temporarily blinded them.

Someone else passed in the corridor, pale-robed, followed by another.

Benedict took the paper back, folded it very carefully along exactly the creases as before, and put it back somewhere inside his jacket.

'Perhaps we should prepare for trouble,' he said with a frown. 'Or at least a degree of inconvenience.'

Vespasia looked at him. She could see no alarm in him, certainly not anything like fear. She turned to Narraway. He was watching the corridors and the people passing up and down it, clearly agitated. Some gesticulated with short, sharp movements, and the buzz of voices was loud, all in languages she did not understand.

'Oh dear,' Benedict said quietly. 'It seems that there is some trouble on the track. Something blocking it. They will have to get men to clear it before we move on.'

'How could that be?' Narraway asked. 'There are no trees to fall, and the land is flat, so a landslide is impossible.' He inclined his head towards the people in the passageway. 'Is that what they are saying?'

'Yes,' Benedict replied. 'Yes. It is something placed there. I think I should have foreseen that. I'm sorry.' The words were without emphasis. It was hard to believe he meant them.

Narraway took his arm, holding him back from going to the door.

'What is the paper you have?' he asked firmly. 'What does it mean, and why should anybody want it badly enough to commit murder for it?'

Benedict turned slowly to stare at him, searching his face as if puzzled that he did not see what he expected.

'You don't know, do you? You really have no idea. I thought perhaps you were just being careful.'

'No, I don't know,' Narraway said tartly. 'But I believe the man who had one like it in Jaffa was murdered in the search for it, and I am beginning to wonder if the same people are now engaged in a deliberate attempt to steal yours as well. They are very similar, but I think not exactly the same. What are they?'

'Together they are two-thirds of everything,' Benedict replied in a tone of voice that suggested the answer should have been obvious. 'But of course, without the last one, they mean nothing at all. With only one of them they have no meaning, no real purpose. But of course you don't understand that, do you.' It was not a question; there was no expectation of an answer in his face, only realisation, and resignation.

'Then where is the third one?' Narraway asked, still keeping hold of Benedict's arm.

Benedict winced and tried to pull away. 'I have seen it, once, a long time ago, but I'm not certain any more. But we must go to Jerusalem. I know that, just as you do.'

'You keep saying that. Is this a literal journey or a metaphorical one?' Narraway persisted.

He was putting into words what Vespasia was beginning to think.

Then a crash of thunder startled her, and she looked out of the window at the darkened sky. There were no more dust flurries or flying sand. It was now all wet, and in the momentary clearing of the glass, she could see little rivulets of water running across the ground.

'Who is it that wants these papers?' Narraway

asked, but he eased his grip on Benedict's arm. 'Who are they? Is it political? Is there going to be some kind of uprising?'

'One day,' Benedict replied with a frown. 'Not yet. Where on earth have you been that you didn't know this?' He peered at Narraway. 'Who taught you? Or failed to. Why are people always looking for uprisings? You want to cure the soul with a sword, and nowadays it's a musket. Have you never read the legend of sowing the dragon's teeth?'

'Yes, of course I have.' Narraway was puzzled and impatient. 'I imagine there was never more fertile soil for growing warriors than here. And I don't want any part of it. I merely wish to take my wife on a journey to Jerusalem, for Christmas.'

Benedict shook his head slowly, as if he were very tired and even more confused. 'That's all most people want. It isn't an option.'

Before he could ask any further questions the door to the corridor swung inwards, the lock successfully forced. Two men threw it open. One was swarthy and wearing a pale turban; the other was smaller with a white face and a striped robe that covered half of his sandalled feet. They looked at Benedict, all but ignoring Narraway and Vespasia.

'You have something that belongs to us,' the turbaned one said barely loudly enough to be heard. 'If you give it back without making a fuss, we will leave you in peace.'

'What I have belongs to everyone.' Benedict looked back with a flash of anxiety stirring his placid features. 'And what you have belongs to everyone,' he went on. 'You don't remember trying to steal it before, do you? No, of course you don't. You go on doing the same thing over and over, and it never works. Does it not occur to you that that is foolish?'

One of the men put his dark, powerful hand on Benedict's sleeve. The other man reached for the curved knife in his belt, his eyes all the time on Narraway.

Vespasia knew with horror what he was going to do as surely as if he had done it already. In her mind's eye she saw blood, and Narraway buckle and slip to the floor. It was unbearable. She had just found him, just learned to love him with a depth she had never allowed herself before.

She gave a loud cry and staggered backwards in the direction of the picnic basket they had brought with them.

Narraway shot her a glance, but he could not

move to help her. The man drew his knife. 'The paper,' he said gently, the word whispered between his teeth.

Vespasia was almost on top of the picnic basket. No one was looking at her. She was an elderly Englishwoman who had fainted at the threat to her husband. Not worth bothering with, at least not yet. Kill, or at least disable the men first!

The blade was shining in the glow of the compartment lamps. It looked almost as if it had blood on it already.

Vespasia straightened up with the bottle in her hand.

Narraway was looking at the knife blade. How quick would it be? Slashed sideways, or thrust upward?

There was no time to think, or to weigh what she was doing. She swung the bottle, heavy, hard, perfectly balanced, and struck the man as hard as she could on the side of his head, below the line of his turban. She felt the crunch as his cheekbone smashed and the instant later blood burst through his skin.

He pitched forward, the knife in his hand just missing Narraway as he went down.

The other man let go of Benedict and lunged at Narraway but he was too late. Narraway bent forward and picked up the fallen knife. He sliced at the man's legs and cut deep. The man let out a strangled cry of shock and fury. But he was bleeding too freely to continue the fight. He grasped at his robes, seeking to tie them tighter, anything to stanch the flow.

His companion lay senseless on the floor.

Narraway climbed to his feet. 'Get out,' he said quietly. 'And don't come back. Benedict! Lift that man off the floor and drag him outside into the passage. Then shut the door and get down that large suitcase off the rack, and jam it as hard as you can to wedge the door shut. The lock seems to be of little use.'

Benedict stared at him.

'Now,' Narraway ordered.

The bleeding man staggered out, still trying to bind his wound, and having enough success probably to save himself. At last Benedict bent over and rather awkwardly dragged the man with the broken cheekbone outside into the corridor. He appeared to be still senseless, but definitely breathing.

When Benedict had finished he closed the door and pulled down the suitcase as Narraway had directed.

All the while Narraway stood with the long, curved knife in his hand, ready to strike if anyone should threaten to attack again. Finally he put it on the seat beside him and turned to look at Vespasia.

Neither of them spoke. They were safe, at least for the moment. If they had ever questioned the importance of the strange pieces of paper with their smudges and lines that appeared to be meaningless, they could not do so now.

If Vespasia had ever doubted that she loved Narraway, and that he also loved her, she could not have married him. But there are depths of believing, of understanding and of feeling. This was a new brilliance of clarity for her. It was too precious to bear parting with, ever. Whatever the price in her own pain, it was worth it.

She turned to Benedict. He must be terribly shaken. It was he they had come for, and had been willing to kill to have the paper, just as they had killed Balthazar. Quickly, silently, and brutally.

Had he known that? Or was this his moment of discovering it?

He looked a little ruffled, and there was surprise in his bland face. Clearly, he had not expected the attack.

Did he even know the value of the paper, or why anybody else wanted it? His answers had been enigmatic, as if it were something he had been told, but did not understand.

'Who has the third paper?' Vespasia asked him.

'I don't know,' he insisted, but there was a slight furrow between his brows. 'I seem to think I knew once, but I can't recall it now.' He smiled. 'But it doesn't matter. He knows, and he will find us when he needs to. It will all be well.'

'They meant to kill you!' Narraway said sharply, his frustration fraying the edges of his temper. 'And they came very close.'

Benedict shrugged slightly, just a gesture. 'But they didn't succeed. Even the bottle of wine is still whole.' He looked at Vespasia with a sudden, sweet smile. 'That is very good. I would not have thought to bring it.'

She wanted to laugh and cry at the same time, and without warning her eyes filled with tears. 'I brought it to drink,' she said tartly. 'Not to hit someone over the head with it!'

'It could be good for both, my dear,' Narraway said huskily. 'We have two glasses, I believe. You and I can share one, and Benedict can have the other.

We should use the respite to fortify ourselves. It is still some distance to Jerusalem. Be sure to keep the bottle . . . and the glasses.'

Vespasia had a vision of what a lethal weapon a broken, long-stemmed glass could be, even more so than a knife, used to its greatest advantage. And if she had doubted it before, she was certain now that the threat was real. Their own safety did not even enter her mind.

She found the glasses and unpacked them. Then she took out a corkscrew. If necessary, it could be another weapon, although it had no cutting edge. She gave Narraway the bottle and corkscrew while she opened a packet with bread and cheese and pieces of fruit. She shared them equally between herself, Narraway and Benedict.

Benedict accepted them without hesitation. He thanked her, but did not mention that she and Narraway had also saved his life. It was odd, as if he did not truly realise what had happened, or the risk they had taken.

They ate quietly while outside, the storm having passed, the last light faded and the winter night closed in. Sunset burned in the west like the embers of a dying fire: a dull, sulphurous red fading into grey, and then black. The only light was that from the carriage windows shining out into the sand and rock, soon blurred as the slanting rain began again. They were islanded, as if nothing existed beyond the train and its passengers. They were all nationalities and faiths, many different races, gentlemen and labourers, soldiers, bankers, shop clerks and farmers. Vespasia had seen them on the platform in the station at Jaffa, overheard conversations in English and French, and of course a multitude of languages she did not understand. They had only one thing in common: they were going to Jerusalem for Christmas. Or perhaps the reason for some was irrelevant: they could have gone at any time.

Benedict did not speak either, but sat motionless except for his apparent enjoyment of the bread and cheese and a crisp apple full of juice. He partook of it with a solemn joy, only occasionally glancing at one or the other of them and giving again that grave smile.

They finished eating and drank the last of the wine, re-corking and saving the bottle. Even eaten in silence and awareness of the other people coming and going along the corridor, it was a strangely companionable meal. Vespasia met Narraway's eyes after and saw a warmth in them as if he too had newly appreciated the sweetness of life and its infinite possibilities.

They had just finished when the train gave a jolt forward. It hesitated a moment, then with a rush of clatter and general noise, it started to move more smoothly and to regain its earlier speed.

Outside the clouds cleared and there were patches of brilliant, almost dazzling stars.

'Do you know where we are?' Vespasia asked.

'More than halfway to Jerusalem,' Narraway replied. 'This journey is six hours. We were nearly four hours along the way when we stopped, three-quarters of an hour ago. If there are no more delays, we will be less than an hour late.'

'I think there will be more,' Benedict said quite calmly. 'It is always further than you think.'

'Jerusalem?' Narraway asked. 'Or anywhere?'

'Jerusalem especially,' Benedict said. 'And then when it comes, whatever the time, it was not long enough.'

'You've done this journey often?' Narraway was surprised.

'No.' Benedict shook his head. 'Never. Nor have you. I know that. But once will be enough. Even if you do it next year too, and every year after that.'

Vespasia was about to ask him what he meant, what part they had in all that was happening. Was it symbolic of a greater whole, something that occurred many times, or only once? Were they at the heart of the journey, or only incidental? Then she looked at his bland, almost expressionless face and decided it would be pointless. His answer was likely to have no meaning for her. The man was gentle-natured, but his mind was different: simple in a way, but detached from immediate reality. His thoughts were in some other realm.

She looked across at Narraway. He appeared to be asleep, but she knew he was not. He was watching the corridor on the other side of the windows and the single, broken-latched door that was their only barrier against the man who had already killed Balthazar and attempted to kill them.

Why were she and Narraway doing this? Was it really just because Balthazar had asked them to, and they were distressed at his death sufficiently to feel they must honour his request? Would they, had they known it was likely to be so dangerous?

Wasn't that a foolish question, when the poor man was murdered in such a way? The implication was obvious, wasn't it? He had all but told them that the paper would be the cause of his death.

And Benedict had shown no surprise at all that he should be attacked. Nor, for that matter, had he conveyed any feeling of guilt for their involvement now, or gratitude that they rescued him. It was almost as if he had expected it.

Had he? Did he know what was going to happen next?

She turned a little in her seat to look at him, studying his face in a way she would normally not have regarded any stranger. It would be an inconceivable breach of manners. It was! But the whole situation was utterly divorced from ordinary life.

If he were aware of her scrutiny, he showed no signs of it. He sat quite still. If his eyes had not been open she would have thought him asleep. He was totally calm, his gaze apparently focused on the empty seat opposite him, as if he would memorise every thread of the fabric. The same slight smile, benign, absent-minded, curved his lips. His blemishless hands rested in his lap, tidily folded, and at ease. Did he understand nothing? Or everything?

The questions that formed in her mind to ask him were absurd. Will we reach Jerusalem? Will there be other forced stops? Who else is on the train, and what do they want? Even: is this real, or am I having a particularly vivid nightmare? Am I really asleep and still in Jaffa?

Or even in London?

They were on this journey because they had been asked to take the paper to the House of Bread on the Via Dolorosa in Jerusalem, by a man they had liked, respected, and who had been horribly killed before he could do so himself. Of course it was dangerous. He had told them so, and the manner of his death sealed the knowledge with certainty. That would be true even if Vespasia had not seen the face of the Watcher in the corridor of the train, which looked and sounded exactly like any other with its polished wood and scratchy seats never at quite the right angle to sit in comfortably. She could have been on her way to Lewisham or Liverpool.

What could the paper be that, completed, it would mean so much?

Was the meaning religious? This seemed unlikely. The whole world already had enough scripture to provide all the answers. It was righteous people understanding the message of hope and peace that it lacked, or of mercy, tenderness, love, however you wished to define that. It was understanding that was short, not words. They were already drowning in an ocean of words.

Benedict spoke of Jerusalem as if it were everyone's goal, but was it? In any sense?

Vespasia had gone to church since childhood. Everyone did. She loved the stained-glass windows, the smell of old stone, certainly the organ with its marvellous, full-throated music, the bells ringing across the countryside. Mostly she loved the passion and strength of the words, the stories of the miracles of man and God.

But was it a balm applied to the outside of her, or the water of life to the soul within? She knew perfectly well what morality she believed, and would live by, whatever the gain or the cost. It grew as experience moulded it, or it changed, but it was never denied. If she betrayed it by deed, she repented bitterly.

But was that anything to do with God, any God that was real, and not the creation of man, in his own image, merciful or punishing, all-powerful or limited by law or logic? Was he loving or merely governing, perhaps understanding nothing of human need or weakness?

She had never asked Narraway what he believed passionately enough to make this sort of commitment to it. Somehow it had always seemed too private a matter to intrude into, like stepping on flowers in bloom, or the new-raked earth of a grave. How could you know, in the silence of the night, what you believed yourself, let alone what anyone else did?

And yet she profoundly wanted to know. Perhaps it would not be too much to say, rattling through the desert night towards Jerusalem and whatever it might mean, that she needed to know at last the beginning of an answer.

Narraway leaned towards her. In this poor light of the shaky lamps, the lines of his face betrayed everything: anxiety, exhaustion, and an over-whelming tenderness she had never seen exactly this way before.

'Sleep a little,' he said so softly she lipread his words rather than heard them. 'I'll watch. Don't argue. I'll take my turn. We should be in Jerusalem long before morning, maybe even before midnight.'

'Should be?' she murmured back. 'Do you think anything in this journey is going to be as we expected?' She said it with a smile. They were on an adventure; why should it be as they had imagined?

'Probably not,' he conceded. 'But there's no turning back. This train goes to Jerusalem, literally and metaphorically.'

He meant it, there was a gravity in his eyes as if he had struggled with some of the same thoughts, and doubts, that she had. This was a journey of the mind, and of the heart, far more than she had ever foreseen. Urgent, frightening questions demanded answers. But this was not the moment to say so. Perhaps he already knew, if not he must come to it in his own time.

She touched his hand very gently. 'My dear, I decided on the journey some time ago. I have no regrets. All journeys go somewhere; perhaps a great deal of the value is in the travelling. I have never seen the desert at night before. The enormity may well be greater than anything else.'

She could see in his expression, shadowed as it was, that he understood all her levels of meaning. She sat back and she closed her eyes.

She had not expected to sleep, but it came unbidden, and almost immediately.

She woke with a jolt so violent she was almost thrown out of her seat. It was still pitch-black outside and the train had stopped as abruptly as if it had struck something on the track.

Narraway was already standing.

Benedict looked a little puzzled, but not altogether surprised. The habitual smile on his lips was all but gone, as he too was staring through the glass at the corridor where several people were gathering. It appeared that they were all men, but as they were in loose robes that reached to the ankles, it was not easy to tell.

'We seem to have hit something,' Narraway said quietly. 'I don't know what it can be. This track is used twice every day, once in each direction.'

'It is because of us,' Benedict told him. 'At least I believe it is. The Watcher is on this train.'

Vespasia froze. He had used the same name for him that she had used, as if he knew as much as they did, although he had not been there.

'Who is he?' Narraway demanded, taking Benedict again and forcing him around until they were face to face. 'If we are to fight him effectively we need to know all we can. I'm not working in the dark any more, playing word games. Who is he, and what is it we are carrying? Why? And to whom?'

'Who is the Watcher?' Benedict turned the words

over in his mind, as if trying to decide exactly what they meant. He looked confused and sad.

Narraway did not help him but stayed with his demanding gaze unwavering.

'I seem to remember that I have known him all my life,' Benedict said at last. 'And yet I am still not exactly sure who he is.'

'That's not an answer!' Narraway snapped. 'I don't want to hear what you don't know. If you expect our help then you owe us the best information you can come up with. You are being totally irresponsible, and we require better of you.'

'Oh dear.' Benedict looked dismayed. 'I dare say you are right.'

Vespasia realised she was sitting with her hands clenched so hard it was painful. Before their marriage, she would have intervened. She would have told Narraway that there was something child-like in Benedict, and a gentler approach would not only have been kinder, it might also have been more productive. But this new relationship gave her both advantages and disadvantages. It had to do with vulnerability, and the power to hurt. Perhaps for the first time in his life, Narraway had allowed someone close enough to him to see his fears, and

– more than that – close to his heart, his needs, his dreams. That was a trust that must never be betrayed.

'Victor . . .' She said only his name.

He glanced at her, then back at Benedict.

'Tell me more,' he urged, but more gently this time. 'Who is the Watcher? I need to know all I can if I am to defeat him.'

Benedict shook his head. 'You will never do that.' He sounded absolutely certain and infuriatingly accepting of it. 'None of us will until the very end. But we can win this part of things, if we are careful.' He smiled. 'Please believe that. I do not tell people everything, but I never lie. The Watcher is a title, not an identity. He can be many people, but always with the same purpose.'

'Which is . . .?' Narraway was keeping his temper with difficulty.

Benedict's eyes widened. 'Oh . . . to destroy, of course. He wants dissension, despair, that rage that kills all that it cannot understand.'

'I see,' Narraway answered as if he understood perfectly. Vespasia thought from his face that he probably did. There was so much that she did not yet know, the horror he never spoke of. The shadow of it was there in his eyes sometimes, awakened by memory of the hot colours of India, the flutter of silks, the sight of a woman with a small child. Only in the last couple of years had she learned that he had studied law at Cambridge, and kept his licence to practise in court. There were so many years between that he rarely mentioned. But Special Branch was a very secretive service; it had to be to fulfil its purpose. She knew he had spent time in Ireland, often doing things he would prefer she never knew about. She had not asked. All full, dangerous and rich lives have learned lessons the hardest of ways, and done things they would prefer to bury along with their regrets.

There were things in her life she would rather he only guessed at, or maybe not even that. There were wounds stitched closed whose threads one did not ever unpick. Let them heal, and the flesh knit together again. The scars were sufficient reminder to keep the lessons fresh. One touched them rarely, and with great tenderness.

'What is it we are carrying?' Narraway turned to another part of his question. 'And what is our part in this whole journey? Are we part of something vast? Do we matter at all, or are we incidental?'

'Oh, no,' Benedict said with certainty. 'No one is incidental, and now, least of all you. It is the answer to the eternal questions.'

'And what are they?' Narraway demanded.

Benedict's eyes widened. 'Really? You don't have questions? Who are you? Do you already know? Or are you so blind, so afraid that you do not ask yourself? Even in the dark, at three o'clock in the morning when the earth is invisible, you do not ask? Or now, in the desert, stranded on a train to Jerusalem, you don't ask yourself, who am I? Where did I come from, and where am I going? Is there any point to it anyway? Did I ever choose this? I don't remember when! Or do you remember?'

'I ask what the hell am I doing here. What am I carrying? And who are you?' Narraway's patience was fraying.

More people came up and down the corridor, some with hands waving, faces angry.

'You are waiting,' Benedict answered calmly. 'Because you don't yet know what to do. A lot of life seems to be like that . . . although perhaps less obviously so than this.'

'And these papers will tell me who I am, what I am, and where I am going?' Narraway asked sarcastically.

'And where you have come from. And, of course, also why!' Benedict said it with absolute certainty.

'And why does the Watcher want it?'

'To destroy it,' Vespasia said, as if it were she who had been asked.

Benedict let out his breath with a sigh, and smiled at her with intense charm. 'Exactly. The lust for power always hates knowledge, just as the darkness hates the light.'

'And who are we taking it to?' Narraway glanced at Vespasia, then back again towards Benedict.

'The House of Bread, on the Via Dolorosa. I have no idea to whom, or why. Only that what they will do with it will be good.'

'I don't think you really have any idea what you are talking about,' Narraway said quietly, disappointment and even pain in his face as the light caught it from the passageway beyond the blocked door.

The outside doors of the train opened and slammed shut. It was not moving, and people were getting out.

Vespasia felt a shiver of fear making the flesh on her arms into goose bumps. She looked at Narraway. If enough people got off they would be alone here, and if the Watcher came back he could kill them with no one to see, or intervene.

'I do!' Benedict protested. 'I don't know the end, but I do know the beginning!'

'And I know the middle,' Narraway said. 'And I am not at all sure that I like it.'

'You knew the man in Jaffa who had the first piece,' Benedict insisted. 'You knew he was good!'

'I did,' Narraway agreed. A sudden sadness was naked in his face, and he was unaware of it. 'And he trusted us to complete his mission. He saw something in us that is either very good, or very stupid, so I suppose that in part only, I accepted his call. We shall take the papers to the House of Bread in Jerusalem.' He glanced at the door again. 'And I think if we are to succeed, we had better get out of here and mix among the other passengers. We can't afford to be trapped in an all-but-deserted train. The Watcher knows where we are, and we have only a bottle, a knife, and two wine glasses to defend ourselves with. Not exactly a great arsenal.'

They left the suitcases behind them, since they were too heavy to carry over the sand, and would serve no purpose anyway. They were well locked, and even the Watcher would not assume they had left the paper he wanted inside them.

Climbing down the carriage steps on to the track was awkward, but Vespasia accomplished it with some grace, and a little assistance. She moved a few yards away from the train, standing motionless in the chill desert air. Only a few wisps of steam rose lazily from the engine into the night. What little light there was shone faintly on the long silver lines of the rails behind them, disappearing around the far side of a shallow hill, its shape almost lost against the further slopes behind it. The air was cold.

She turned and looked ahead. The last steam evaporated against the darkness and was lost. She could barely make out the shape of the engine. All that was visible was the rounded top of its roof, and the outline of the funnel. Its bulk, its power, even the arches of the wheels were lost in the density of shadow.

She lifted her face to look up at the stars. How would anyone follow one star to Bethlehem? Or anywhere? The whole sky blazed with them, countless millions, like the sands of an endless ocean, burning silently outward to the many edges of infinity. If that was the creation of God, what could all the doings of man matter to Him in the least?

Were there other worlds out there? Life? Other beings with hopes and dreams? Did anything else laugh, like man? Create music, love each other, and write their names in the sand for the next wind to blow away?

The other passengers were gathering into groups, talking to each other. There were all sorts of people, men and women, some clearly families, standing close together, the men protecting the women, although nothing threatened them, except possibly the desert itself, if they could not get the train started again.

Without the sun, there was no colour. Everything was shadows of grey and black, impenetrable. Some men wore turbans, making their heads look huge, and yet oddly graceful. Long robes fluttered a little when the breeze stirred. It was ice-edged, and made an odd whispering in the sand. It seemed never to be still.

Vespasia gazed around and could see no vegetation. Perhaps in the daylight there would be grasses of some sort, but now the desert appeared lifeless, like the rubble of some giant lost city. Men had walked this land since the time of Abraham. Of course they had done so much longer, but that was long enough ago for the imagination. He had had herds of animals. There must have been grass somewhere near, and water.

Benedict was standing beside her, also staring at the sky. Even in this very dim light, she and Narraway were close enough to him to see the expression in his upturned face. It was a look of awe so deep it would have been irreverent to interrupt him.

Finally he turned to them.

'The wind is not strong, but it is cold. Many people are sheltering on the leeward side of that slight hill over there. It may not be more than a few feet high, but it must be enough to break the wind's edge. If we are here for long that will matter.' And, without waiting for their reply, he began walking slowly towards the outcrop. He was an odd figure, in his pale Western suit and elegant boots. He moved not awkwardly so much as carefully, as though uncertain of the ground beneath him.

The terrain was stony, uneven, exactly as it must have been for thousands of years. The only sign that man had even passed that way was the silver-grey parallel lines of the railway track, and of course the huge train sitting like a dormant beast of some sort.

The air was clear and cold, and it smelled slightly bitter, as if someone had trodden on a pungent herb.

Narraway looked around.

Vespasia knew what he was seeking: some official from the train service to tell him what the problem was that had stopped them this time, and when they could expect to remedy it. Perhaps they would have to wait for another train to come for them, from Jerusalem.

If there ever were another train? Either way, they could not be left stranded here.

'I wonder how close we are to Jerusalem,' she said. 'If they can't get this difficulty solved easily, perhaps they will send some other form of transport for us. I hope it is not camels! I do not think I should ride a camel well.' She said it ruefully, half as a joke.

Narraway put his arm around her and she felt the warmth of him with a quick pleasure. It was not something he would have done in the daylight. After a long time, in many senses alone, physical affection was something he was becoming accustomed to only slowly, quite delicately, and with a joy she found deeply touching.

They walked towards the head of the train, and

the engine. Presumably that was where the trouble was, either with the train itself, or with the track.

Narraway looked from one side to the other. The landscape was almost flat. The moon was just visible rising in the east, a day past full, and it was becoming easier to see as the pale, silver light spread. It was extraordinary how beautiful it was, even without a trace of colour.

'There are no bluffs, no escarpments anywhere near here,' Narraway said gently. In the desert night sound carried easily. They could hear the murmur of voices almost a hundred yards away. 'There's nothing rocks could have fallen from, and no heavy drifts of sand. Probably why they took this route. It has to be the engine.'

That was not good news. A broken part would almost certainly have to be replaced.

'If they haven't got another engine of some sort, they'll come here by other means,' he went on, turning slowly to look along the tracks both before and behind them. 'We can't be far from the nearest town. The line has been going for years. It won't be the first time it's broken down,' he said with, Vespasia felt sure, more certainty than he felt.

'Perhaps they will bring a herd of horses, and we

shall all ride into Jerusalem, as they must have done in the past?' she suggested, only half flippantly. She was tired and frightened. It was getting increasingly difficult to keep a steady voice and not let the edge of despair become a reality.

They reached the engine and found a man in a railway uniform. He was covered in dust and oil, and he was struggling to maintain his composure.

'Sorry, sir,' he said politely. 'We are not quite sure what the problem is. Doing the best we can to find it, then we will be able to mend it.'

'You carry spare parts?' Narraway said, more as an observation than a question.

'Of course. Very good railway. Very good. My apologies, sir.'

Narraway thanked him, then together he and Vespasia walked slowly back past many of the other passengers, looking for Benedict again. He would be easy to see in his pale jacket and trousers. Almost everyone else was either in dark clothes, or in the sort of robes worn by both men and women who lived in this region and climate.

'I can't see him,' Vespasia said after several minutes. 'What can have happened to him? Surely he wouldn't wander off into the desert? What for?

If he wished to use the facilities he would have done that before leaving the train. Could he have gone back there?'

'It's possible,' Narraway agreed reluctantly. 'He doesn't seem to have much real appreciation of his own vulnerability. He's . . .' he looked for a term that was applicable, '. . . a sort of holy fool,' he finished. As he said it he took her arm again and started back towards the train, looking at the carriages to recognise the one from which they had come.

'Would he find the same one?' she asked, struggling to keep up with him. Her legs ached and she had very little energy left. 'He could be in any.'

'We'll start there,' he replied. 'I have no idea what he recognises, or doesn't.'

'Do you think he's in danger?' she asked anxiously. She wanted him to say no, and yet if he had she would have thought only that he had not recognised the truth, or that he was no longer being honest with her. That would be worse. It would leave her in an isolation she knew would be the deepest loss she could experience. Only now, with trust so strong between them, had she understood how alone she had been in the deepest sense. Only in the sharing of passions and dreams, above all the tenderness of shared pain, the hungers that invade the soul, did real intimacy lie. Physical intimacy was a small thing beside it, sweet and intense as it was.

They were at the doors to their carriage. It was a high step up because it was built to get into from a platform, not from the ground beside the rails.

'Of course he's in danger,' Narraway said quietly. 'Balthazar had the first drawing, and they killed him. Benedict has the second. They will kill him if they have to.'

'We have the first one,' she reminded him. 'In the corridor, when I met Benedict, I saw the Watcher too. I was alone with him for a few moments and I looked into his face. He knows we have it.'

'You should give it back to me,' he said. 'I mean it, Vespasia. Apart from anything else, the value of your life or mine, I have a better chance of defending it.'

'And probably a better chance of getting to Jerusalem and delivering it,' she agreed. 'At least if this were a physical battle, or one of endurance and knowledge of such things. But I don't believe it is. Do you?'

He turned to search her face, but they were in the

shadow of the train and the moonlight was hidden.

'What do you think it is? Are you going to say "a battle of the spirit"?' There was amusement in his voice, and fear. The laughter was at his own vulnerability.

'I don't know. But whatever it is, we will do it together, or not at all. Please stop being heroic, and just be sensible.'

This time he did laugh. 'I'm not in the least heroic! I served so long in Special Branch precisely because above all things I am a realist. Heroes have their place, and the world needs them. They inspire us all. Without them we become completely pedestrian, with our feet stuck in the mud and, too easily, our hearts as well. But in the secret wars against treason and betrayal, the hidden weapons of doubt and terror, it is being clever that counts, not just honourable and brave.'

'You are not in Special Branch any longer,' she pointed out.

He winced. She barely saw it in the shadows, but she knew it because she felt, always, how it hurt him, no matter how he pretended it did not.

She had said it because she truly meant what followed it.

'You are free to be heroic again,' she told him. 'The detached pragmatism was the clothes you wore, not who you were.'

'I feel a trifle naked,' he said drily.

She had no answer that was appropriate to the situation.

'Please give me a hand up into the carriage, and let us see if our holy fool is inside,' she asked instead.

He hesitated only an instant, then reached up and grasped the door handle. He opened the door a little awkwardly, then swung it wider and climbed up. He turned back to help her. She was hampered by her skirts but, after a moment's difficulty, she stood inside and they closed the door.

At first they heard nothing. Then gradually there was the sound of leather against leather, as if someone were moving suitcases.

'That's our compartment!' Vespasia whispered. 'He's in there!'

'Benedict?'

'No! The Watcher.'

Then a moment later they heard Benedict's voice.

'You are making a mess, and it is quite pointless, you know.'

'I can destroy it all! Then the picture will be destroyed too.' It was a strange, raspy, sibilant voice and yet, for all its oddness, extraordinarily human. Vespasia could recognise the emotion in it as if it had touched her skin. It was rage.

'Of course you can,' Benedict agreed. 'You can destroy anything that has a physical being. But you can't create anything. You gave that up, of choice, remember?'

'I remember everything! It is you who have forgotten!'

'Not entirely – not everything,' Benedict answered, as if the fact surprised him.

'I can destroy you!' the Watcher said in reply, and Vespasia heard relish in his tone now as if, in some disgusting way, he could taste flesh in his mouth.

'No, you can't.' Benedict did not seem afraid.

'I can make you destroy yourself!' the Watcher hissed back.

'Only if I let you,' Benedict answered. 'And I never have yet.'

The Watcher's voice was confident, high in his throat. 'This is different, oh so very different! You have no idea yet, no idea at all. I can hurt you in ways you cannot even imagine. You are a fool! A dreamer. A child who has learned nothing yet. But you will find out.'

Narraway took Vespasia by the hand and held it almost too tightly, but she did not pull away.

'Maybe,' Benedict agreed. 'But I can learn.'

'You don't even know why you are going to Jerusalem!' The Watcher gave a bark of laughter, and yet it was an infinitely human sound, with all human anger and pain in it.

'I know it's a good reason, and that's all that matters,' Benedict answered.

'You fool!'

'Perhaps, but it will be only temporary.' There was a kind of smooth certainty in Benedict now, as if the matter were already decided.

Vespasia gripped Narraway's hand that was still holding her arm. She felt his fingers tighten even more.

'I can't touch you, but I can kill others, others you care about,' the Watcher all but snarled the words. 'That's your weakness: guilt and shared pain. I killed the man in the Jaffa hotel room. He saw me, he knew I was coming, but there was still nothing he could do to stop me. All his wisdom was no use to him then. And all your innocence will be no use to you.'

'But you didn't get the picture, did you!' It was not a question. Benedict's tone, the wording, oozed satisfaction. 'We're nearly in Jerusalem already, and you have none of them.'

There was a sound of a blow, flesh striking flesh, and a cry of surprise and pain from Benedict.

Narraway let go of Vespasia and charged forward, bursting the carriage door open. She followed on his heels, and saw, in the moonlight coming through the compartment window, the black figure of the Watcher with his hands around Benedict's throat. He was taller by several inches, and seemed to be much stronger.

Narraway struck the Watcher a blow with all his weight behind it, catching him on the neck with the side of his fist.

The Watcher lost his balance and fell sideways. Narraway hit him again, and he doubled up and struck the armrest with a sickening crunch.

Benedict appeared stunned. He clambered to his feet, seeming a little dizzy. For an instant, he looked at Narraway with amazement, then he turned to the Watcher and shook his head.

'This is all so stupid,' he said sadly. 'He will hurt so many people.' He shuddered. 'So very many! But in the end he will never win.' He frowned and closed his eyes.

'Come on,' Narraway urged. 'We have to leave here. He may come around quite soon, and he will be even more dangerous.' He took Benedict's arm. 'Come on!' he ordered more sharply.

Benedict opened his eyes and, even in the moonlight, Vespasia could see a new fear in his face. 'At least I don't think so. I always believed he would not.'

Narraway ignored him.

'Why?' Vespasia asked. 'Why don't you think so?' She could see that it troubled him, robbed him of the confidence he had possessed before. 'Benedict?'

'I thought he couldn't win,' Benedict answered her. 'But perhaps if he hurts enough people then he will. Do you think?'

'No, I don't.' She said it with a certainty she wished she felt.

'Of course you're right.' He shot her a smile she could see even in the shadows, the whiteness of his teeth caught in the light for an instant.

On the floor, the Watcher stirred.

Benedict charged out of the door and into the passageway, with Vespasia behind him and Narraway behind her. They did not stop until they were out of the carriage, and standing on the hard-baked dust and stones of the desert floor.

The train was still motionless. The huge arch of the sky stretched to infinity, burning with stars. The other passengers were quiet, huddled together in groups, the night consuming their voices until they seemed to be silent, making no more sound than the wind moving the particles of sand from one surface to another.

'Where's Benedict?' Vespasia said softly when she had turned her attention from the stars. She looked around, but he had disappeared into the shadows. 'I can't see him.'

'The Watcher is behind us,' Narraway replied. 'Benedict will be all right, at least for the time being. And at least now he knows the danger he's in.'

'But does he believe it?' she asked, starting to move forward. 'And even if he does, we need to find him. He has the second part of the picture.'

'I know. And more to the point, I think he has a far better idea than we do as to what it means. I think he will find us, even if we don't find him.'

'Do you?' She doubted it. She was seriously concerned that Benedict was too innocent of human nature to have more than a vague idea of the behaviour of those without scruples, the greedy and the violent whose own needs always come first. Or even of those who are too deeply frightened to take up weapons against people they know are stronger than they are.

They moved among the groups of people close by, some standing, some taking the chance to sit. Several times they stopped to ask. Benedict was easy to describe. His clothes alone made him stand out. Some people were happy to point one way or another, others shook their heads and looked blank.

Vespasia and Narraway moved from one group to the next, always staying close together, and repeating their enquiries.

'Of course he could be moving too,' Vespasia pointed out. 'Even just ahead of us. Perhaps we should go back to the train.' She did not like the idea of returning to the compartment, but the Watcher would not have remained there. And even so, once the train started to move again, it was possibly less than an hour to Jerusalem.

'We had better go back,' he agreed. 'No doubt Benedict will be making his way back too.' He looked around. They were on the very outskirts of the crowd. Many people seemed to be waiting, heads lifted hopefully. The night was definitely growing colder.

A belch of steam shot up from the engine, and several of the passengers cheered.

It was short-lived. People ahead of them stopped. The darkness seemed more dense, the silence heavier after the flare of hope.

Other people kept trudging forward, determined to believe. Or perhaps they only wished to shelter in the carriages to protect them from the chill wind, which was getting stronger.

Vespasia searched the crowds for the pale, trouser-clad figure of Benedict. Twice she thought she saw him, but it turned out to be someone else.

Then in the shadow of a rocky outcrop some distance from the train she saw the dark figure of the Watcher. She knew beyond doubt that it was him by the curious lope of his stride, as if he had no weight, and yet he could not easily get his footing on the sand.

And ahead of him she saw Benedict. This time she knew it was him. He had his back to the Watcher and his attention seemed to be on something in the distance.

The Watcher was closing the gap between them, his shoulders hunched, his head bent forward.

Narraway acted before she did.

'Benedict!' he shouted at the top of his voice. It

echoed from one rock face to another until it seemed to come from all directions, even though the inclines were wide and shallow.

Benedict turned. He saw the Watcher and raised his arms.

The Watcher stopped.

Narraway started forward, moving quickly from Vespasia to keep up with him.

Benedict seemed to be carrying a stick. He had been using it to lean on as he walked, but from the way he swung it now, it was heavy. Was he actually prepared to fight? The Watcher was still motionless. Then he began to turn very slowly, as if searching for something in the distance.

With a touch like ice, Vespasia knew what it was. He had seen Narraway, and he was looking for her. She was the weak spot, the place where he was vulnerable. That was what he meant when he had told Benedict that he would hurt others. If you care at all for anyone, anything, there were always hostages to fortune.

She could not hide. The escarpments were shallow on the windward side, too bare to shelter anyone, too steep for her to climb easily, even if she were not hampered by skirts. Their sharper faces were in the opposite direction, too far away to offer any cover.

If she ran towards Narraway she would cross closer to the Watcher and be an easy target. If she ran back the Watcher was still closer to her than Benedict was. He would reach her first. For a long, terrible moment she was paralysed by indecision.

Then at last Benedict moved, surprisingly swiftly, running towards the Watcher, going to come between him and Narraway, cutting off his path to Vespasia. He clutched the stick as if he meant to use it.

Narraway turned back to block the Watcher's retreat.

Benedict caught up with the Watcher and when he was still a few yards short of him he hurled the stick and it caught the Watcher with surprising accuracy, sending him sprawling on the ground. It was an attack from the one direction he had not expected.

Narraway reached the stick and picked it up. From the awkward angle at which he held it, Vespasia realised it was extraordinarily heavy, like ironwood.

Benedict reached them and stood still, looking down at the black-robed body crumpled on the ground.

In the distance the train engine belched steam

again and there was a loud clang, then another, then more steam. Slowly the engine started to move, to gather speed and travel away into the night.

They stood stunned as it disappeared, leaving only the starlight on the empty track.

For moments no one spoke. Vespasia felt a wave of utter desolation overtake her. She was so tired her whole body ached. With an effort she kept her head high. She must not let them down. Narraway believed so much of her!

It was Narraway who broke the silence. He did not pretend.

'I doubt anyone will miss us, at least not until the train gets into Jerusalem. And perhaps not even then. If they do, they'll send someone back to search, I presume. Either way, we would be better off moving. It is still quite a long time till sunrise and we will be very cold indeed if we stay still. There's nothing here to burn for a fire, even if we had the means to light one.

'If we follow the tracks we will not risk getting lost, and we will be as much on the level as possible.' He looked at Vespasia. 'I'm sorry. This is not what I intended.' He said it wryly. His serious moments came in times of happiness, or the perception of beauty. When facing danger he did so with slight, very dry humour.

She must not let him see how lost, how defeated she felt. He would blame himself.

'Our biggest need will be water,' she replied. 'But one hopes we can manage without it for a few hours. Long enough to find habitation, or possibly a stream or a pool of some sort.'

Benedict looked puzzled. 'This is a turn of events I did not foresee,' he admitted. 'Still, victory must be possible.' He did not explain why he thought so, but looked at the track stretching west towards Jaffa, and then turned slowly and stared to the east, still dark, towards Jerusalem. 'I suppose we had better begin. Sometimes I wonder why on earth the plan seems to keep changing. I don't suppose you know, do you?' He looked automatically at Narraway.

'Plan?' Narraway began to walk, keeping pace with Vespasia. 'I hadn't perceived that there was one.'

'I think you are joking,' Benedict answered. 'I've noticed that about you. When things are confusing or unpleasant, you make jokes.'

'It's an English thing,' Narraway replied, still watching the stones ahead of him rather than looking at Benedict. 'It's how we deal with our fears . . . or griefs. Make bad jokes, or laugh at nothing at all.'

'Very odd.' Benedict shook his head. 'But I suppose I shall have to get used to it. In fact, on giving it consideration, I think I may come to find it comfortable, even admirable.'

Narraway smiled, but he did not answer.

For some time they concentrated on walking steadily beside the track. It was fairly level and mostly sand, shale and small stones, not difficult terrain compared to the alternatives.

For what seemed a long time no one spoke. They saved their strength for walking.

Vespasia felt her mouth was dry, and knew the others would be aware of the same, but there was no help for it, so not to speak of it was better.

The moon rose higher and shed a silver glow over the endless sea of desert, with its old river beds, and the shadows of the few stark trees, winter-blasted.

After a good hour, Vespasia stopped for a moment and cast a look back over the way they had come. Five hundred yards away she saw as he crested a rise, the black figure of a man, bare-headed, his long robes flaring outwards with his movement.

She did not need a second look to know who it was: the Watcher, somehow risen from the insensible heap on the earth that they had left only a short while ago. With sickening certainty she recognised the purpose in his gait, and the speed.

'Victor!'

He looked at her, hearing the sharpness in her voice, then he followed her gaze and saw with a stiffening of alarm exactly what she had.

'Benedict! We must prepare to fight. We can't outrun him. What weapons do we have?'

Benedict was alarmed. Clearly he had not expected the Watcher to come after them. Whether he had assumed he was dead or not was another matter. He stood motionless, his face bleak, almost mask-like.

He seemed to make a great effort of thought, and of will.

'Perhaps I should give you my paper, and then go towards him,' he said quietly. 'He cannot go in two directions at once.'

'I don't agree,' Narraway said after only a moment's hesitation. 'No one person should have both pieces of paper. An all-or-nothing tactic is likely to end in nothing. This way we neither win nor lose. Losing matters very much, doesn't it?' It was a genuine question. Neither he nor Vespasia had any idea of what real significance the papers had.

Benedict looked around him in all directions, a touch of panic in him now. It was the first intense emotion Vespasia had seen in him, and it was alarming. Nothing before had actually frightened him.

The Watcher was significantly closer.

'Is there any point in keeping moving?' she asked. 'He can outpace us, I'm afraid. But what weapons do we have, other than your knife, and Benedict's staff?'

'I must protect you,' Benedict seemed to have reached a decision. 'He can wound me, but he can't kill me. He can kill either of you, or even both.'

Argument now was pointless, or asking for an explanation of such an absurd statement. So also would any attempt be at running away. They stood a little apart, Vespasia in the centre between them. Narraway had his long, very slightly curved knife in his right hand, although getting close enough to the Watcher to use it might be already fatal. Benedict held the long staff in both hands.

Vespasia had no weapon, but then anything less than a gun would have been no use anyway.

What a ridiculous way to die! Marooned in the

desert somewhere outside Jerusalem, and for the sake of a piece of paper whose meaning – if there were any at all – was too obscure for them to understand.

The Watcher stopped about fifty yards from them. In the faint light they could not see his face, but they knew him from his unusual posture and the swift, odd way in which he moved.

He seemed to be staring beyond them, as if they were too close for him to see clearly, even though it was still at least fifty yards.

Very slowly Vespasia turned to see where his gaze was focused. Then she understood. Approaching them over the rough ground, but still soundlessly, were a dozen horsemen. They too wore long robes, which fluttered in the wind, but they also had head coverings of some sort. It was impossible to be certain, but the fabric of their clothes was more varied in shade. Their horses moved at a walk, but they did not stumble or hesitate. The gleam of the moonlight on steel showed the men were well armed.

As Vespasia stared at them, they increased speed very slightly. Another spur forward and it would be a charge.

A horse snorted and there was a rattle of hoofs on stone.

Narraway swung around also to face them and Benedict stayed with his staff ready in case the Watcher should make a sudden lunge at them.

One horseman held up his hand, halting the others, then he rode forward as Narraway faced him.

The man was turbaned, dark-bearded.

'Salaam,' he said politely.

'Do you speak English?' Narraway asked him. 'Or French perhaps?'

'English,' the man replied with slight amusement. 'And Arabic, and Hebrew, and Farsi. You seem to have encountered some unpleasantness. May we be of assistance?'

Narraway had to make an instant decision. To be seen consulting with Benedict would make him appear weak. To consult with Vespasia would be unthinkable.

'Our train from Jaffa broke down, and unfortunately when it was mended it went on without us,' he explained. 'Now we are obliged to walk, and are about to be attacked by a robber.' He gestured towards where the Watcher was fast approaching.

The horsemen beside him fanned out a little and drew their swords.

Vespasia glanced around her, and saw that the Watcher was only thirty feet away, but he had stopped. Even if he thought himself invincible, he knew he could feel pain, could be rendered sense-less, where he would be vulnerable to any attack, if only by whatever wild beasts or carrion animals might roam the desert.

'We will take you to shelter,' the leading horseman offered. 'And food. You must need rest. We are not far from Jerusalem. It will be an easy journey in the daylight. Come.' He looked at Vespasia, then back at Narraway. 'I'm sure the lady has walked far enough.' He was obliquely asking for Narraway's permission to take her on his horse.

Of course she had walked more than far enough. Her whole body ached and her feet were rubbed raw with sand grains inside her boots. They were designed to be comfortable, but not for desert hiking.

Narraway did not hesitate. 'Thank you,' he accepted. They all knew that any alternative was better than remaining in the desert to face the Watcher. Even if they survived that encounter, it still left them to walk the unknown distance to Jerusalem, possibly wounded.

The horseman rode forward and reached down to assist Vespasia up on to the saddle in front of him. She could have ridden behind. She was a good horse-woman, but he could not have known that.

Others also rode forward and Narraway and Benedict were assisted up as well, in their cases to sit astride behind the riders.

The Watcher was closer, but other horsemen moved forward, long, curved scimitars drawn. Within moments they turned to ride with gathering speed over the hard, flat earth towards the east.

Vespasia had no idea how long the ride was. It seemed closer to two hours than one, but eventually they arrived at a large building in the centre of what was a well-watered and civilised area. However, she could see even in the fitful moonlight that it was all one estate rather than a town.

They rode into a kind of courtyard where torches were burning, giving a warm glow, and there seemed to be several men waiting for them. They took the horses, assisting Vespasia to dismount and rearrange her skirts before being conducted into the paved and firelit outer room, and then further inside again to where a group of people awaited them.

Their leader was immediately apparent. He was

a tall man, and she guessed he was in his late forties. His thick, dark beard was untouched by grey, yet there was maturity to his features and deep lines of character, powerful and mercurial. She guessed he was a man used to being obeyed. He was dressed in plain robes, but there was gold on his hands and around his neck. He introduced himself with a long name beginning with 'Haroun'.

'Welcome to my house,' he said warmly, looking at them each in turn. 'My men told me that your train broke down, and then unfortunately when it was mended and started again it was remiss enough to have left you behind? And then some wandering robber pursued you? Allow me to offer you the hospitality of my home and redeem some of the shame of my country that you should be treated in such a way. It is not our custom, I assure you.'

Benedict looked tired, dirty and uncomfortable. He allowed Narraway to speak for all of them.

Narraway was also exhausted and filthy from not only tramping across the desert country but also fighting with the Watcher, but he appeared not to be disconcerted by it.

'Thank you,' he said with considerable dignity. 'I am afraid we are much in need of help. We must be in Jerusalem by the eve of Christmas, and although it is not far, I believe, we have no means of travelling, except to walk.'

'Of course. First you must eat, and then rest.' Haroun was smiling now. 'Then we will accompany you into Jerusalem. You must allow my men to do that much for you. Unfortunately there are robbers on the road.' He gave a very slight shrug, the gold on his hands and wrists gleaming in the light. 'Especially at this time of the year when there are so many pilgrims around. It is most regrettable.'

Haroun was an excellent host. Although it was beyond midnight, he ordered a delicate and refreshing meal for them, and plenty of both wine and water.

'Tell me about yourselves?' he invited them, leaning back in his chair and regarding them one by one. His eyes lingered on Vespasia with interest. He must have wondered what an Englishwoman of once fabled beauty, and now past her prime years, would be doing on foot in the desert in the middle of the night. What reversal in her fortunes could have occasioned such an event?

Benedict did not seem to interest him so much. Compared with Narraway he was bland, and too young to have much experience. He was nondescript, neither dark not fair. There was nothing within his face except bewilderment, and now also weariness.

'Are you pilgrims?' Haroun enquired.

Vespasia looked at his face. From his expression he was interested; it was not merely polite conversation. It was clearly Narraway he was addressing, so she did not answer. She wondered how Narraway would answer. If she had been asked when they left London, she would have answered that they were not. The idea would have amused her. Were she being asked now, she would have been far less certain. Were they indeed pilgrims? Disciples in a faith they really knew only in outline and ritual, but not in the soul?

As though prompted by her thought, Narraway answered.

'Are not we all explorers, pilgrims of one sort or another?' he said with a smile. 'The difference between us is the point at which we realise it.'

Vespasia looked at him with a tenderness that overwhelmed her. Was he saying that for himself? Or had he somehow understood it in her also? Or was it for both of them?

Rather than being put off, Haroun seemed to be more interested. He studied Narraway's dark face for some moments, then he looked at Benedict, and back again.

'An old city, Jerusalem,' he said thoughtfully. 'Where is it you go? To the City of David? The West Wall of the Temple he was not permitted to build because of the blood on his hands? Or the Dome of the Rock, where Mohammed ascended to heaven? Or the Via Dolorosa, along which Christ carried his own cross?'

Narraway smiled at him, and took a sip of the excellent wine. 'Perhaps I go to the Mount Moriah where Abraham paid his tithes to Melchizedek, on his way to Egypt, and later was prepared to sacrifice his beloved son Isaac,' he said thoughtfully.

Haroun gave an answering smile. 'I think perhaps you are a diplomat, sir, carefully choosing the middle ground: Abraham, the father of all three of the great Western religions. You are safe with that.'

'You make him sound indecisive,' Benedict cut in. 'A man of no specific commitment. We respect all, but we hold our own beliefs.'

Vespasia was surprised to hear him speak of all three of them as if their opinions were one.

Narraway did not respond.

Haroun looked at Benedict. 'So you go to all

equally, no one is against you, and no one is for you! Who was the robber in the desert who followed you so assiduously?'

'An evil man,' Benedict said softly. 'A man who has failed in his unhappy existence.'

'He was very strong, and very angry,' Vespasia spoke for the first time. She was quite aware of the decorum required of her that she did not argue or contradict the men, indeed that she should not speak unless invited to. But she would not allow Benedict to speak for her, as if he had that right.

Benedict looked surprised. 'Is that not the greatest of all failings, to allow your anger to use your strength in abusing others? Strength should only ever be used for good. The abuse of power is man's greatest failure, is it not?'

'What a strange person you are,' Haroun said with quickened interest. He studied Benedict's face, as if examining it would enlighten him. 'There is pity in your voice . . . and yet the man would have robbed you of whatever little you have, even your lives! Or, of course, he might have held you for ransom for whatever wealth he imagines your families to possess?'

'I have only the wealth we all have,' Benedict told

him. 'Except perhaps knowledge. Yes, I have knowledge he does not, because he does not believe it. He does not understand.'

'And you do?' Haroun turned to Narraway. 'And you do also? You look like a man who has wealth. Your clothes and shoes are of good quality. Your wife also wears fine clothes. I know something of the beauty of Western women, and I see she is exceptional. Maybe he wished to hold you for ransom?'

Vespasia felt a shiver of discomfort. She was so tired that the room took on a hazy quality, as if the distances between one table and another were more than they should be. The walls, the exquisite pillows were moving, yet she had no more than sipped the wine.

'I doubt it,' Narraway replied, seeming to speak casually, and yet Vespasia was aware that he was choosing his words with the greatest care. 'When I had office, that would have been worth someone's time. But not now. We are simply travellers, like any other, wishing to be in Jerusalem for Christmas.'

'The three of you?' Haroun asked.

'My wife and I, yes. Benedict must answer for himself.'

Haroun looked at Benedict.

Benedict's smile was sweet and gentle. 'Oh, yes. It is every man's purpose, whether he knows it or not. We are fortunate in that we know it.'

'How do you know?' Now Haroun was the charming and interesting host again. 'You speak with such conviction. Someone you believe has told you? Ah . . . better than that, you have seen a sign?' He smiled back, showing wonderful white teeth. 'I know your legend of the star that shines over Jerusalem . . .'

'Bethlehem,' Vespasia corrected him.

'Yes . . . Beit Lechem. That means "the House of Bread", you know? But tell me, how can a star shine over one particular place? We have a saying, you cannot step into the same river twice, meaning that the water flows and is never the same. The earth turns. How do you follow a star, except it be at the Pole?'

Narraway gave the question some thought, and this time Benedict remained silent.

The answer formed itself slowly in Vespasia's mind, and by the time Narraway spoke, she was as certain of it as if she had said the words herself.

'It is not a vision in the sky.' Narraway measured his reply. 'As you say, it would appear to us to move, as the earth turns. This is perfectly steady, a certainty within you that the thing you are looking for is blemishless, a light by which all other things can be seen for what they truly are.'

The interest in Haroun's face changed from polite attention to a swift, keen, single-minded concentration.

'Indeed!' He let out his breath slowly. 'If that is so, then I understand why you walk the desert at night in such a fashion. It would be a treasure beyond any price. Other men might well attack you, if they were aware you sought such a thing. Why do you take your wife with you? The danger will affect her also: that you must have considered. Or did you think that no others would know it, and you would pass simply as pilgrims, two among the thousands of others?'

The idea of being no more than camouflage did not appeal to Vespasia, but she knew it would be unwise – and, to Haroun, unseemly – for her to speak now. But she saw the flash of anger in Narraway's eyes. Would he tell Haroun that she had as much courage and intelligence as any man? Or that she was the daughter of an earl, an English lord of high rank, and not accustomed to being treated with disrespect? Or even that the wealth was hers?

He chose simply the one truth that mattered. He did it with a smile.

'The journey was my Christmas gift to her. At the outset I did not know of this . . . star. But then at the beginning of any journey, who knows where the end will be?'

Haroun smiled back and there was a glint of appreciation in his eyes. 'That would be a journey well worth the making,' he agreed. 'But all the same, this is perilous. Did the robber who so closely followed you know that you have seen such a star?'

'I have only the evidence I have told you,' Narraway replied. 'Certainly he seemed to think we had something worth his attention – and risk. Twice already we have fought with him. But he may imagine my wife has jewels.' He left the suggestion hanging.

Haroun looked at Benedict. 'And have you seen the star also?'

'Oh, yes. I have followed it a long way. And the Watcher has always been not far behind.'

'The Watcher?' Haroun said quickly. 'That is the man in the desert who followed you so assiduously?'

'Yes.'

'He has attempted before to steal it from you?'

'You cannot steal a belief,' Narraway interrupted before Benedict could give away more.

'Yes, you can,' Benedict would not be silenced. 'Weariness, fear, disillusionment with what you had thought, before the greater understanding comes to you, physical pain, loneliness, loss – all can take away your faith to press forward. The star is not always visible. Sometimes for all the straining of your eyes, you cannot see it. All you can do is remember where it was, and keep travelling.' He stopped suddenly, as if finally realising that he had said too much.

Haroun was looking at him intently, the beginning of a new comprehension in his face.

Vespasia was overcome by a wave of tiredness. The food had sustained her a little, and temporary safety from the Watcher, but they still had far to go, if not in miles at least in achievement. And they had not yet found the third piece of paper, without which the two they had made little sense – in fact none at all.

'Tomorrow is the Eve of Christmas,' she said gently, looking at Haroun. 'We are deeply grateful to you for rescuing us not only from the robber, but from the cold of the desert night, the hunger and thirst, and the possibly insurmountable difficulty of walking the rest of the way to Jerusalem. Perhaps after a little sleep, you will be kind enough to direct us in the rest of our path?'

'Of course.' His manner of the host returned again. 'You need somewhere to rest, so you may arrive at the correct time.' He rose to his feet. 'But I would be lacking in my duty, and my privilege as your host, if I allowed you to make the rest of your way unguarded or unprotected. In the morning you must rise and eat, and then my men will accompany you to the city gates. It is not far. You will arrive safely, and well in time to keep your appointment with Destiny.' He smiled. 'I will ride with you. No! Don't try to dissuade me. This is a journey of all mankind. It is only right that I come with you, and make it myself. It is a privilege.' He inclined his head a fraction, the nearest he would ever come to a bow.

Vespasia did not need even to glance at Narraway. They both knew it would be not only discourteous but dangerous to try to refuse him. It would also be pointless. They had accepted his help when they were in great danger from the Watcher, and from the desert itself. The obligation was overwhelming.

'Thank you,' Narraway said gravely, his expression indefinable.

Benedict actually seemed pleased, as if he could see only the advantage of having a man of such rank with them. Vespasia could not help thinking that he was naïve to a dangerous degree. Whoever had entrusted to him such an important undertaking? And where was the third piece of the puzzle? What manner of person would be the keeper of that? Please heaven he was still alive . . . Or she? Could it be a woman? Probably not.

They slept deeply for what remained of the night, then after a light breakfast they set out in the dawn. There was a brief discussion as to whether Vespasia could manage a horse herself. She gave the impertinent man a look that should have frozen the sweat on his skin, and was permitted a gentle mare, which she accepted with more grace than she felt. She had ridden since she was a child, and very well.

They left the huge estate and rode out along a worn and level track that nevertheless quickly disappeared into sand and loose shale. The air was cold and smelled of stone and dust, with a faint aroma of bitter herbs. It was exhilarating, as if it held a promise of something utterly new. Vespasia breathed in deeply, and felt herself smiling. She ought to have been exhausted still, but instead she was excited.

The dawn was pale in the east, giving enough light so no animal stumbled, but it was delicate, all bleached colours almost without substance. A slight wind stirred, shifting the dust between the stones, too soft to make any noise.

Then suddenly the sun rose above the horizon, brilliant, a white fire in the sky that painted the landscape with borrowed colours, purples and peaches and gold. Shadows were dark, umber, almost black. There was an illusion that one could see for miles, every rise and fall of the land, every buttress of rock or ancient, gnarled remnants of a tree.

The day took its own shape again. The air of new birth was swallowed up in the journey.

They began to talk. There was no longer any spell to be broken by conversation.

'Now there is daylight and we can see.' Haroun was the first to speak. He was riding beside Narraway and Vespasia, and ahead of Benedict. 'Are we then equal, or does this star within give you power still?' He was smiling to rob the remark of offence, but there was curiosity in his voice.

Narraway chose to play it lightly. 'I'm afraid not. We are still dependent on your grace to get us to Jerusalem. We owe you both our means of transport and our guidance. Away from the railway tracks we are blind.'

'But safe,' Haroun pointed out. 'Your Watcher no longer knows where he can find you, nor could he vanquish you even if he did. Is that not the better choice?'

'Certainly,' Narraway agreed. 'Anything we could accomplish in Jerusalem is pointless, if we do not get there.'

Now Haroun's smile showed his white teeth. 'And you trust me to get you there! You are a man of great faith.'

Narraway was not a man to trust in faith at all, and Vespasia knew that. He was a man of deep knowledge and skill, and great judgement of men and usually of meticulous planning. He could hardly have led an organisation like Special Branch, defending the country from its secret enemies within and without, were he to rely on faith of any sort. But she had no wish for Haroun to know that Narraway was what to him would be termed a spymaster.

And of course this had nothing to do with Special Branch. They were on a private holiday, a journey intended as a gift, an exploration peculiarly appropriate to this time of year. Christian in values, perhaps, but not in any spiritual sense. At least that is how it had begun.

Perhaps the journey to Jerusalem was one of discovery more than anything else. What would she learn of this complicated man she loved, and perhaps knew far less of than she had thought? What would he learn of himself? Maybe that was an even greater question.

They had had little chance to speak to each other except when someone else was present. And even during the small part of the night when they were private, they were both too tired to stay awake long, and very aware of Haroun's men, and a few women servants, in the corridors.

Perhaps most importantly, there had been no chance to ask Benedict where he thought they might meet whoever would have the final piece of the picture.

Was Narraway a man of faith after all? Or was it simply that there was nothing else left to cling to? There were no facts beyond the existence of the two papers, the goodness of Balthazar, his wisdom and his death, the Watcher following them and now unquestionably attacking them. Everything else was a feeling, an unbreakable will to do something because someone was also determined to stop them.

There was no star in the astronomical sense; it was an inner vision, perhaps an imagined one created by people who felt compelled to see sense in things, a purpose, whether none existed.

Haroun was riding ahead with Narraway now, but Vespasia could hear a little of their conversation. It was about power. She heard a snatch of it from Haroun, his voice carrying.

'It is only power if you can use it,' he argued. 'What is this treasure you seek, what is this star leading you towards? Is it simply knowledge of some belief within yourself?'

Was he speaking of religion, or of politics? Is that what it was really about, underneath the talk of faith?

'Don't insult me, Haroun,' Narraway replied. 'You know as well as I do that no power is of value if you have not first learned to govern yourself. Power is also responsibility. The yielding of power to someone else can offer great relief, even freedom. You no longer have to excel – no burdens, no expectations. If there is no success, then there can also be no failure. That is the ultimate peace for some.'

Haroun laughed, a harsh sound. 'I am insulting you? You are no more a man like that than I am. I can see it in your face, the lines, even around your eyes. You need to find whatever the star gives you, even at the cost of dragging your wife into discomfort and at times danger. She follows you because she has little choice, and perhaps she is accustomed to obedience.'

This time it was Narraway who laughed, a sudden sound of rich enjoyment against the wind and the soft thud of hoofs in the sand.

Vespasia knew what he was thinking. On the rare occasions when he was disposed to give instructions she obeyed because she loved him, never because she had not the strength or the courage to do otherwise. She hoped fervently that he would have more wisdom than to say so now. She did not want Haroun's disapproval; even less did she wish his interest. The thought was peculiarly repellent.

'She knows her place,' Narraway replied. How very ambiguous that remark was! It could have meant anything. Perhaps Haroun had forgotten that England was ruled by a woman, as was a quarter of the world in the British Empire.

'We shall ride with you all the way to Jerusalem,' Haroun said. 'We must make certain that you are safe. Perhaps even as far as your destination. It is an ancient city, crushed with people, especially at this time of the year. If this Watcher of yours is ahead of you now, then he may be waiting for you in the crowds as they pass along the streets. Or in the shadows of the narrow alleys, the archways, the steps between one passageway and another.'

Narraway did not reply.

'Does this faith of yours tell you that you are invulnerable? That you cannot be harmed?' Haroun persisted. 'Are you a man chosen above all others by whatever God you believe in, so that the hands of lesser men cannot prevail against you?'

'Certainly not,' Narraway said without hesitation. 'I think the mission is as much for me as for mankind. Certainly it is not for God.'

Vespasia listened to him with surprise, but at that moment she did not care about considering his beliefs. She was not thinking of the purpose of their journey, or even of Balthazar for whom it had cost so much, but of Narraway and the danger he was in because he intended to see it through, whatever it meant. It did not really matter whether it was out of faith in the religious or spiritual sense, or only the determination to keep the promise Balthazar had asked of him. He must know the danger he was in. The Watcher had tried twice to kill them. Now Haroun's hospitality had saved them, but she didn't know why, and to what end.

They rode east into the brightening morning, the sun now high enough to cast sharp shadows on the desert floor. Vespasia was certain that Haroun and his men were not only their escort against another attack from the Watcher, their guide to the gates of Jerusalem, and their easy and swift transport, they were also their gaolers. As long as they were mounted, and in the centre of the group as they rode along the way east, it would be impossible to break free. His men rode swift horses; they were used to the desert; they were all armed with scimitars: long, curved and razor sharp. There had been no threats. They would be completely unnecessary. It was all there in the silence: the grace, the ease in the saddle, the never-resting eyes.

Narraway and Haroun were talking again of faith

and power. Haroun could not let it be. Perhaps he already knew what the papers meant and he was testing Narraway. Or was he determined to find them, including the last piece, and put them together to gain some greater power than he already possessed?

'Knowledge,' he said thoughtfully, looking again at Narraway. 'You say it is some kind of knowledge? But knowledge is no use unless you can use it. You have no power if people do not know you have it. Power to do what?'

'I don't know,' Narraway admitted.

Vespasia could not see his face because she was riding just behind him. She wished he would change the subject. Haroun was dangerous. Perhaps the whole quest was dangerous. They had begun it simply to keep a promise to a man they had admired. They had thought it little more than an errand.

No, that was not true. By the time Narraway had found the paper, he knew Balthazar had been murdered for its sake. He had looked at the strange marks that looked like neither picture nor writing, and he had believed it mattered. He had seen the inner star that he had spoken of to Haroun. Maybe now he was looking for an answer of his own, a faith in something he believed was there to be found, to be understood.

She was afraid for him, afraid that he would be hurt, perhaps even killed. And she was also afraid that when he arrived in Jerusalem he would find only an ancient city full of passion and complexity and the roots of three great faiths, but not any answers beyond the ones that each person brought with them anyway. Perhaps it was not in any sense a destination of the spirit. Was that a delusion that would cut to the heart, discovering an emptiness as deep as any pain?

But no matter what she thought, she must not interfere. Love does not bind others to its own need.

She looked across at Benedict and saw nothing in his face but patience.

They were climbing very slightly, and as they reached the top of an escarpment they turned and looked at a different view, invisible before. Spread out ahead of them lay the holy city of Jerusalem. The light gleamed on the golden Dome of the Rock, but Vespasia's eyes searched for and found the ruins of the Temple of Solomon amid the roof-tops of the ancient city through which Christ had walked. At the end of the road ahead of them the crowds of people, traders and beggars milled around the high walls and the huge, magnificent Jaffa Gate.

As one, the riders stopped, all struck with emotion as if they had never seen it before, although Haroun's men must have seen it countless times.

No one spoke. Each one could have been as alone as if no one else had ever sat here on horseback and viewed the city for the first time in his or her own special way.

Vespasia looked at Benedict. What did he see? The City of David, and of Solomon? Or, older than that, the Mount where Abraham was willing to sacrifice Isaac to the will of God?

What did Narraway see? She looked at him and thought with the gravity in him that maybe it was Gethsemane, or Golgotha, and she was afraid for him. But she must not interfere, even if she could.

What did she see? All those things. And yet as she stared at the hillside, the rooftops, the trees, it was another garden she was looking for: the one in which Mary Magdalene was the first mortal to see the empty tomb and the risen Christ.

It must be in one of those spaces where there were trees. Did it matter which one? No, it did not matter in the slightest if she never saw it. She knew it was there.

She urged her horse forward a little, and at the very same moment Haroun did the same. As one body, as if impelled by a single urge, they all began to descend the very slight incline and move towards the main road. No one spoke.

Vespasia wished she could have been alone with Narraway. They could have talked of what they felt, what they hoped for. But then, they had expected to arrive by train, in the new, modern way as befitted the turn of the century and the dawn of a new age.

This was the way they might have come since time immemorial. In fact, they would part from Haroun, one way or another, and in the end go on foot, in the oldest way of all.

But how could they escape Haroun and his men? That was now the most pressing question.

They continued in silence. The last thousand yards or so of the sand was level and easy, smoothed by uncountable feet coming this way over the millennia, all seeking, and perhaps each one finding something different, or possibly nothing at all.

As they drew closer to the Jaffa Gate itself, a vast monument towering into the air above them, Vespasia and Narraway saw it was bigger than they had imagined in the distance. It was massive, built of stone hewn out of rock so long ago it did not seem man-made. And yet clearly it was: built of desert-coloured pale rock, perfectly proportioned. It had narrow slits in its height – not windows, but ports for the defenders to shoot arrows from – and giant gates within that would be closed at night.

The crowds around the outside seemed oblivious of it, like ants moving purposefully in the dust, now and then a moment of bright colours of reds and blues in a robe. Most clothing seemed practical, dust and rock-coloured, with occasional black or dark brown, purple as shadows.

Old men had long beards and stood philosophising, arguing, bargaining. Women sold food and water. Children played, held fruit or sweetmeats, laughed and cried. Dogs looked hopefully for scraps. Camels waited with occasional impatient complaining sounds too clear to be misread.

Haroun and his men dismounted. Narraway, Benedict and Vespasia did the same. Half of the men took the horses to care for them, see them rubbed down, watered and fed. A desert man cares for his beast before himself. It is not altruism, but survival.

Without his horse he is dead, and he has known that since childhood.

Haroun looked at Narraway, briefly including Vespasia. He inclined his head towards the vast archway of the gate rising into the air like a castle beyond the milling, noisy crowd outside. It was clearly an invitation.

Would Narraway agree? Was it all over without even a struggle?

Vespasia turned to look to one side at a woman who was selling bright silks set out on a flimsy stall. She took a step towards it.

One of Haroun's men took a step in the same direction, his eyes on her.

She stared back angrily, as if he had touched her.

He did not move. That in itself was a statement.

Benedict backed away as if frightened, and collided with a woman carrying a bale of cloth. She lost her balance and dropped the bale on to the ground, then turned angrily to berate him for causing it to be soiled with dust.

Someone laughed. A quarrel broke out and a dog seized its chance to steal a piece of fried meat. The quarrel became more heated and other people joined in. The woman whose meat had been taken shouted at the dog's owner and several other dogs joined in the general mêlée.

Vespasia felt Narraway's hand on her arm, impelling her forward. It was the best chance they were likely to have. They plunged ahead and then turned quickly, not to run in a predictable straight line.

Every route seemed to be blocked. They twisted and turned, trying always to find their way back towards the gate, and not to be herded against the wall where there was no escape. They passed through close-packed crowds and then open spaces. They saw men who could have been Haroun's. Most men looked alike in their soft, earth-coloured robes with flashes now and again of white. Some wore turbans, and others were bare-headed.

Vespasia was breathless, her heart pounding. She was almost at the great shadowed end of the gate when she saw a boy, perhaps ten or eleven, standing wide-eyed and filled with fear. He was staring straight at her as if begging her for help, knowing it would not come.

Then a hard-faced man seized him from behind and gave him a stiff blow around the head. The boy's eyes filled with tears of pain.

Without giving it a thought, Vespasia strode

forward and snatched a stick from an old man nearby. She swung it as hard as she could at the man who had hit the boy, knocking him off balance. Narraway lunged forward to take her arm and pull her away, but she was too angry to yield. She gave the stick back to its owner, then she opened her purse and shook out all the money she had. She threw it to the ground in front of the man, who was now climbing to his feet again. He looked across at the coins on the ground, then at her.

Narraway sized up the situation and acted out his part. He grasped the boy by the hand and pulled him forward. Surprisingly the boy came without any protest.

There was no time for argument now, or for Narraway to tell her what he considered of her action. Together, and closely followed by the boy, they ran for the gate and into the shadow.

At the far side they emerged, Benedict beside them, puzzled, but his face shining with victory. They were in Jerusalem.

'Hurry,' Narraway said briskly. 'They won't be far behind us.' He turned to the boy. He had no idea what language even to try. He had no Arabic at all, or Hebrew. The boy was thin, olive-skinned and with huge dark eyes. He could have been of any Middle Eastern race, or even Southern Spanish.

'Will you be all right?' Narraway used English. Since it was at least the most common tongue in the world, it was a place to begin.

The boy nodded gravely. He looked at Vespasia and smiled, a slow, sweet expression of great gentleness. 'Thank you, lady,' he said. His voice was husky, perhaps on the edge of breaking into the beginning of manhood.

'You are welcome,' she said equally seriously.

'We must move,' Narraway warned them. 'We are still too near the gate. Haroun will find us here.'

The boy still looked at Vespasia. 'I have something for you,' he said. 'It is . . . precious.'

Vespasia shook her head. 'You don't need to give me anything.'

He took no notice of her. He pulled out of his meagre clothing a piece of parchment rolled up and flattened, and passed it to her, watching her face.

She took it and opened it up, her fingers trembling. She knew what it was the moment she saw even the beginning of it. It was the final piece of the treasure they were looking for, and she saw at a glance that this was in Latin. With time, they would be able to decipher it, even though the writing was hasty and distorted by emotion. She met his eyes, solemn and warning.

'Thank you,' she answered him, folding it up again and putting it inside the front of her dress where it was invisible. 'What is your name?'

'Jeshua,' he replied. 'Please be careful.'

'I will. Are you coming with us?'

'Yes.' It was just one word, and yet it held intense meaning. He said it with certainty and the shadow of a smile.

She took his arm and they walked together a step or two behind Narraway and Benedict as they followed behind the other pilgrims. It was Christmas Eve, and the Via Dolorosa was the destination of many.

They stayed together as closely as they could, but it was a long walk and they were jostled and pushed. Everyone was excited. Some were weeping as if close to hysteria. Others were angry. There was an electricity in the air that Vespasia found disturbing. The emotion was out of control. There seemed to be fierce, loyal and intensely bigoted people pressing forward, ready to fight anyone who challenged their views. Some had faces distorted by anger. Others were made beautiful by piety. They were all ages, all races, both men and women.

Vespasia clung on to Narraway, afraid of losing him in the press. Jeshua walked beside her. Benedict pushed the way open before them.

She looked for any sign of a bakery. The street was narrow and winding. There were steep stairs in the passages between one house and another, and archways across so that people could go from one side without touching the street, unseen by those below, and pass to the further side.

There were shops, houses, alleyways that led off to courtyards. People stood in the shelter of doorways, watching. All humanity seemed to be here, searching and expecting.

Then suddenly it was there, a narrow door with the sign reading that bread was for sale. Was that it? The House of Bread? Beit Lechem!

No one else seemed to be taking any notice of it. They were pressing on with their journeys, eager to have walked the whole distance, expectant of some crowning emotion at the end.

Narraway saw the sign also and pulled her into the doorway. It was Benedict, a step ahead of them, who pushed on the worn, wooden door and felt it yield under his hand.

Inside was a small shop, a single counter and behind it an ancient man with a white beard covering most of his wizened face. He smiled at them and nodded, looking carefully at Benedict, a man with such an innocent, unmarked face, and the foreigners. Lastly he looked at the boy, and his smile widened until it was radiant.

'Upstairs,' he said clearly, in English. He pointed to another, rather battered door. 'No one is here yet, but you are welcome.'

'Thank you,' Narraway replied, and led the way up a steep, winding stair. It was past midday already.

At the top was a room with a large wooden table and many chairs. They went in and closed the door. Narraway looked, but there was no lock on it. Nor was there any other way of entering or leaving.

Vespasia knew he was wondering if they dared take out their pieces of parchment and look at them. And yet if they did not, what was the purpose of having accomplished their journey? They had risked so much to keep them safe and bring them here. Why did they have them? What would it tell them, now that it was what was purported to be the end of the journey? If they passed them to someone else without looking at them themselves, they would never know what the secret was, the knowledge for which Balthazar had given his life, and the Watcher had followed him from . . . where?

Benedict reached into his inside pocket and placed his piece, open, on the table.

Narraway carried his, which he had taken back from Vespasia to keep, for her own sake, and set it down beside Benedict's.

Vespasia took the last one which Jeshua had given her and laid it down also.

It was Jeshua who read them slowly, his voice hoarse with emotion.

I was walking in the evening among the cypresses and I met a man to whom I confessed the guilt that had burdened me since the crucifixion I ordered of the heretic who thought himself the King of the Jews. I knew it was political expediency that condemned him, not any sin, and yet I agreed to it.

The man spoke to me gently and explained why it was necessary that Jesus be put to death. It was part of an eternal plan in the mind of

God, and must needs be. He made me feel that I was forgivable, and that is surely the sweetest thing any man can hear. And as he smiled at me, I knew him, and the next moment he vanished from my sight.

I, Pontius Pilate, of all men, have seen the risen Christ, and walked and talked with him, as if I had been his friend. This I swear.

And it was signed at the end.

Jeshua moved to the next, and read it more easily. It was not in Latin, but in Aramaic, his own tongue.

I remember the light in the room when the Angel of God told me that I would bear a son who would be the Messiah all time had waited for, and he could be the son of God. And so it came to pass.

When he was eight days old, so small in my arms, so vulnerable, the prophet Simeon saw him and knew who he was, and that the salvation of the world was in him. And yet he told me also that a sword would pierce my heart because of it.

And that too came to pass. I watched him

grow and loved him. But when they betrayed him and denied him, I could not help. I stood at the foot of the cross they nailed him to, and I waited with him till the end.

It had to be. This I understand now, and he lives. I held him in my arms again, just once, and I know the glory of God. His love is for everything that lives and it has no bounds. His purpose is sure and eternal. This I know, because I, Mary, was permitted briefly to be the hand-maid of the Lord.

And it too was signed.

Without looking up at them, Jeshua read the last.

When I was a young man I died, and was buried three days in the tomb, my flesh beginning to rot away. In my spirit I saw God, and He showed me his existence in the spirit of all men, and then their mortal lives, frail, beautiful, brief and so precious. Lastly He showed me the eternity of joy that was possible in the path of courage and love. Man was created a god in embryo. Time has no end, and love has no boundaries.

It was my destiny to return, to be called back

to earthly life to show forth the power of God over death, over all darkness and despair. I cannot make you believe this, but I, Lazarus, above all others, know this to be true.

It also was signed.

Narraway breathed out slowly and his voice was husky when he spoke. 'What does it mean?'

'It means that man was born of the spirit in the beginning of time,' Benedict answered.

'And will be resurrected, into the eternity of his choosing,' Jeshua added. 'To live for ever, loving and creating without end.'

'And in between?' Narraway said. 'And what do you mean, "of his own choosing"?'

'I think he means that "in between" is the time of choosing,' Vespasia said. 'That is life on earth. The time when we choose between courage and cowardice, honour and lies, love or the denial of passion, hope and faith. Perhaps most importantly, to forgive. Without that there can be no real love. It is not one choice, it is a million small ones, between light and darkness.'

'Is it?' Narraway looked at her curiously, trying to read in her face what she meant, if she were guessing or if she thought she knew. 'Where is God in this? Or the power of evil, Satan, or whatever you want to call him? What you are seeing is only man.'

'No . . . I think . . .' She searched for what she did think, for what the words were saying. Why did it have the power that had caused the Watcher to want it so desperately that he would murder Balthazar for it, and Narraway and Vespasia also, if he could, even Benedict? What did he not want them to know?

She looked at the documents again. This was the simple, passionate faith at the heart of all Christianity: real people, walking through life with the dust of the road on their feet, not scarlet slippers, not embroidered robes, not a gold cross but a wooden one, with blood soaked into it. Above all, love. A wave of loss almost drowned her and darkness filled the room.

Narraway's hands gripped her so tightly pain shot through her limbs and she had to pull away. She heard his voice saying her name, roughly, harsh with fear.

She forced herself to open her eyes and look at the papers again. There was something infinitely precious in these words.

Slowly her fear slipped away. 'It's a journey,' she said quietly. 'The path is endless, but it is one path. We are not separate, we are merely at different stages of a journey that has no end. And one stage should not hate or despise another, not fear it, nor envy it. It all looks so clear . . .' She turned to Benedict. 'You are the one who knows why the beginning . . .'

Benedict nodded, the wide, innocent smile on his face.

She looked at the boy. 'And you guess the future, or perhaps you know something of it?'

'I have seen,' he answered. 'Little bits. Beautiful, like shards of an infinite light.'

'And what are we?' Narraway smiled ruefully. 'No, don't bother to answer. We are the middle, the bit that doesn't remember the beginning and barely imagines the end. We are the bit that clutches at shadows and is torn apart by hope and fear.'

'I'm afraid, my dear, we are the bit that is the fulcrum upon which it all turns. We are the ones who decide what heaven will be.'

Narraway was aghast. 'Good God! For all of us?'

'No, of course not. Just each for ourselves. We decide because each one of us knows what it is we wish to pay the cost for.'

'Who do we give it to, this . . . this testimony from the past?' he asked.

'To the Wise Men who are meeting here tonight, I imagine,' she said. She looked at Jeshua.

'I think so,' he agreed. 'This is the House of Bread – Beit Lechem. We have followed our inner stars, and this is where they have led us.'

'There's no one else here,' Benedict pointed out.

'Then we wait,' Narraway said, as if he would settle the matter. He fished in his pocket and brought out a few coins. 'We have food for the soul. Perhaps downstairs in the bakery they will sell us some bread for the body.'

It was early evening when the first visitors arrived. The shadows were already deep and the sky pricking through each moment with new stars. They could see it through the large window to the room, and even though it was to the side rather than the front, the sounds of shouting and chanting came up from the street.

There was a sharp rap on the door and before anyone could answer, it was thrust open. A man in a dark robe held it for another, older man to come in.

'Thank you, my friend,' the second man said quietly. Then, as the door closed, he moved into the candlelight, which was also provided by the shop below. He had a long white beard and his eyes were oval, black, deep sunken and bright with interest. He regarded them with benign surprise, particularly Vespasia. There did not appear to be any emotion in his look.

Narraway introduced them, simply by name and without explanation. The three papers were folded up and out of sight.

'I am a minister,' he answered. 'My name does not matter.' He looked at them with a keen interest, studying their faces first, then the marks of travel on their clothes. 'I see we have all come far,' he observed.

Narraway offered him bread and wine, also from the bakery, which he accepted.

It was not long before there was another knock at the door, and the same dark-cloaked man let in a second visitor, again without speaking.

This man's clothes were also to his ankles, but not an Eastern robe. It was more like a Western churchman's cassock, although it was a rich purple shade and excellent cloth. If it denoted anything, it was that he was a bishop, although there was no gold cross around his neck, nor gold ring on his finger.

'Cardinal?' Narraway asked curiously.

The man inclined his head. 'Indeed. It seems there is only one of us left to come. Who are you?' He looked at the minister. 'There is no ill news, I hope?' There was a shadow of concern in his face.

'Faith, my friend,' the minister said gently. 'Evil walks abroad but it has always been so. This is still a new beginning.' He turned to the boy. 'Jeshua?'

'Not yet,' the cardinal cautioned.

Neither of them seemed disturbed by the presence of Narraway or Vespasia, and they were almost unaware of Benedict, who watched them all with a benign, happy bewilderment.

'Jeshua?' the cardinal said again.

The boy smiled, but did not reply.

Vespasia was aware of a gathering emotion in the small, upper room with its one-way view over the rooftops of the city. Who else were they waiting for? When he came, what would then happen? Would those who had brought the papers be allowed to remain? Or were they only messengers?

It was Christmas Eve. The stars were brilliant, as

if the sky were pierced to let through some greater light beyond.

There was a knock at the door and the servant opened it without waiting for anyone to answer, and ushered in the last visitor.

The Greek Orthodox bishop was a fine-looking man, tall and proud. His face was ascetic but gentle, as if a lifetime of self-discipline had taught him both his own weaknesses and those of others, and he had pity on all of them.

The three men greeted each other with clear affection, and then asked Narraway for the papers.

They set them down carefully and looked at what was shown. In each of their faces was awe.

'The faith as it should be, that we have lost in our own pride and lust for dominion. The path of man,' the minister said for all of them. 'Beginning with Mary and her acceptance, even when she could have no idea what it would carry her through. Then the fire of knowledge, for all of us, step by marvellous, agonising step, walking in faith, struggling to believe. Then at last we cross forth into eternity, our true selves, children of God ready at last for what it will bring. Seen in these words, it is so clear.'

The bishop smiled, but there was a sadness in his

eyes. 'So clear indeed. I look at him once and he is Orthodox, like me. Then he is a Protestant, like you, then a Catholic like our brother here. He is black, or white, he is of the ancients in the Americas, or of the East. He is a man, or a woman, every woman, with or without child, young or old. He . . . she . . . is God's child, and that is all that matters.'

'And this terrible and beautiful earth is our path,' the bishop added. 'If only we could treat it with the love and the nurture it deserves.'

'It is all so simple,' the cardinal said sadly. 'Love the great God who made it, by whatever means you will. Honour all that He has made, and love your fellow man. Treat him with gentleness, forgive his mistakes as you would have God forgive yours, and all else will fall into its rightful place. The rituals you choose to help your path are nothing. Do what guides or eases your way. Do not deny me my own, as if they appear foolish to you.'

The bishop smiled. 'For that, my brother, we must accept that they are the way, not the end.'

'I know . . . I know!'

'We are slow to yield that our identity is not the essence of who we are.' The minister gave a rueful shrug. 'We have been a peculiar people for thousands of years, persecuted for it, feared for it, hated because hate is easier than understanding. We have paid with too much blood and pain to give up that which was so dearly bought.'

'For all of us,' the bishop agreed. 'We too were born in sacrifice. Now when we are free to do as we please, we risk fading like a ghost, and in the end dying of apathy.'

The cardinal nodded. 'What we gain too easily we too often do not treasure sufficiently to keep. I sometimes wonder if our mothers love us as their own lives because we entered it from their pain. But you are right, we are paying now too much in other people's pain. There is enough in mortal life; we do not need to add to it.' He held out both his hands and for a moment they each clasped the hands of the two others.

'The picture is clear,' the minister said, breaking the silence. 'We are all the men in these testimonies, or the women, if you will. It is all of us by journey from the infant in spirit, through faith to take our mortal life with all its doubt, pain and danger, at last to become gentle, brave, and with the beginning of wisdom to embark on an apprenticeship to God himself. If we can teach this, a step at a time, we will build a core of love and belief that will forgive ourselves and others, and we shall conquer the darkness.'

'It will be hard,' the bishop said, shaking his head. 'Pride wants to lead, not to follow.'

The cardinal shrugged. 'We say that the love of money is the root of all evil, but I think it is really pride, the fear of change, of attempting something at which we may fail. The evil one would have us court safety, and follow the lesser path.'

'Of course,' the minister agreed. 'He sows fear in the mind. But we have chosen this journey. Let us press forward.'

The bishop looked at Jeshua. 'Thank you,' he said fervently. 'I give you my word we will do all we can.'

'I know,' the boy said with a smile.

One by one the priests all thanked him, then Vespasia and Narraway, then lastly Benedict.

It was Vespasia who asked the question that she and Narraway had been thinking since the first parchment was given to them by Balthazar. 'I see now that it is the journey of all men,' she said quietly. 'A choice before this life, typified by Benedict. More choices in mortality . . .' She gestured to Narraway and herself. 'And Jeshua is the future, the resurrection, if you like. All that is yet to come. But who found these, and where? Why were they hidden at all? The knowledge should belong to everyone. It always should have.'

'It has,' the minister answered her. 'Abraham knew it, and untold men before that. Perhaps Eve knew it when she accepted the knowledge of good and evil, and opened the door for all of us to take a complete life, with all its chances, sublime and terrible. It is given when there is someone who will use it for good more than for evil. I do not know who decided this particular way of sharing it, but these papers were found in the desert many years ago. They were barely discovered when some pursued them for gain, some for fear of a knowledge that could plant doubt, or disobedience in the hearts of some. These are the people who cling on to power in the belief that they alone should have knowledge; that it is too dangerous for the common man. And at times they have been right – but it is not their decision to make.'

'Light is for the world,' the cardinal added, 'not for the self-chosen few.'

There was a loud bang downstairs, as if a door

had been flung open so hard it had crashed into the wall beside it.

They all froze.

'The enemy has come,' the bishop said quietly, his face ashen. 'We have too little time.'

'It is as we feared,' the cardinal agreed. 'We must take these and keep them until—'

Whatever he had been going to say was cut off by shouting below and more crashes, as if furniture were being overturned.

Vespasia looked at Narraway.

'There's no way out,' he said gravely. 'We must fight. I have a good knife. What has anyone else?'

'We do not carry weapons,' the bishop answered, his face bleached of all colour.

'There is a way through the chimney and on to the roof, and there to the next house,' the cardinal said.

The minister started to move towards the empty hearth. He looked at Narraway with profound respect. 'I loathe leaving you thus, but the documents must be saved.'

Narraway did not hesitate. 'Go. We'll hold them as long as we can.'

Vespasia felt a lurch of fear, then of pride, and a

great warmth inside herself. She would sacrifice her life with him, and he had no need to ask her. He knew her well enough to be certain. Perhaps that was the ultimate acceptance.

The bishop clasped Narraway's hand with a grip that made him wince. 'We will continue to work secretly to bring all men into one sacred journey. If we do not meet again in this life, we will do so beyond.'

The priest saluted them with a tiny gesture, then they all three went into the hearth and through the hidden door to the side of where the fire had been. They were followed immediately by Benedict. Only Jeshua turned and looked at them with tears in his eyes. Then he, too, was gone.

Narraway looked at Vespasia once. It was too late now to touch or kiss, or say any of the myriad things that were still to be said between them. They had to be understood in one glance.

The door crashed open and the Watcher stood there, his face a mask of rage, his eyes like burning holes in his head. He had missed the two men who separated the past and the future, and, more than that, he had missed the three men who would carry the message of eternal hope for the unity of

Christendom, and perhaps one day for all mankind. He had only the present – the man and woman of today – from whom to exact his vengeance.

His staff was long and heavy. Vespasia saw now that its end was cased in iron, sharp pointed and already covered in blood where it rested on the wooden floor.

Would he come for her first, and have Narraway watch while he killed her? No. It would be the other way around. He would not turn his back on the man with the knife. She would have to watch, then he would take his time with her, his pleasure in pain and above all, fear.

Yet for all that she understood, it was his killing Narraway that infuriated her! She reached for any kind of weapon at all, anything that would distract him so Narraway could use the knife, even once.

The fireplace! Was there anything there for when it was lit? A poker, tongs? She saw none. The window was glass. But she had nothing to break it with. Could she hit it hard enough with an elbow? She'd probably only break her arm.

The Watcher moved forward very slowly, always towards Narraway. Would he speak here, demanding to be given the papers? Narraway was watching him, waiting for the lunge. Vespasia could see it quite clearly now: he expected to die, but as long as he took the Watcher with him, he would not mind. They were in an upper room. He was prepared to go backwards out of the window, away from Vespasia, away from whatever he could do to her that would be a slow and terrible death.

That was who he was. There were a hundred things about him she liked, but this was the core that would in the end give everything for what he loved and believed.

He was standing now with his back to the window. The Watcher was half sideways, still so he could whip around and attack Vespasia if she came too close, if she had some weapon after all.

Narraway moved the knife as if to strike.

The Watcher gave a low laugh in his throat, a terrible, animal sound, and lashed out with the staff. Narraway ducked and he missed, but not by much. One contact would kill.

They were very close to the window now. In its dark glass their reflection blurred as one, lunging and whirling to evade and strike again.

Vespasia searched desperately for anything with which to lash back at the Watcher. She could see nothing at all. The room was bare. He was moving closer to Narraway, driving him towards the window, each blow with the staff missing by less.

There was nothing for her to do but launch herself at his back, catching hold of his robes and dragging all her weight to throw him off balance. He missed Narraway and struck the wall near the window and the jolt of it came back through his arm, tugging at his shoulder. He staggered, losing the perfection of his balance. His reaction was a fraction of a second too slow. Narraway lunged forward with the knife and it struck flesh.

The Watcher screamed, not with pain but with fury that he had been cut. Ignoring Vespasia as if she were nothing, he drove at Narraway with all his weight and strength. Narraway stepped sideways and ducked down and the Watcher hurtled forward, dragging Narraway with him, and locked together they smashed through the window scattering glass shards into the night, and fell with the Watcher's cloak floating out like wings. They crashed into the crowd of pilgrims jostling along the street amid howls of fear and anger.

Vespasia stood gazing at the space where the window had been, trying to peer into the darkness at the crowd below her in the Via Dolorosa, everyone pushing and stumbling their way towards Golgotha.

It was seconds before she could see Narraway struggling to get to his feet.

'Thank God! Thank God!' She all but choked on the words, not knowing if she said them aloud. She turned and ran to the door and down the stairs.

The bakery was deserted, the street was crammed with people, but she forced her way through them, not caring who she pushed aside or who else's feet she trod on, as she made her way to the pavement below the window.

There seemed to be glass everywhere, but she ignored its crunching under her feet. She found Narraway dazed and having difficulty keeping his balance, but upright. The Watcher was on the ground, his body smaller than she would have expected. His own staff skewered his chest and leaned at a crazy angle, as if the next person to knock into it by accident would lay it flat, unintentionally making the gaping wound even worse. All they were aware of was the emotions, the passion and tragedy of the place that all history had steeped it in.

She clasped Narraway in her arms and felt a wave of relief engulf her, as he held her as if he would never let her go.

The wave of people passed them. Vespasia and

Narraway leaned against the wall of the bakery and stared up at the sky. The noise ebbed away and for all they knew, or cared, there could have been no one else there. The sky was bright with stars, and as they stared upwards more blazed suddenly, wildly, across the arc of heaven, brilliant lights that filled the darkness, and then disappeared again beyond the horizon. But those that saw them would never forget what they had seen.

DISCOVER MORE FESTIVE
MYSTERIES FROM THE INIMITABLE
ANNE PERRY

DISCOVER THE
WILLIAM MONK
SERIES

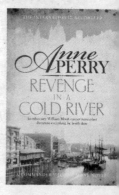

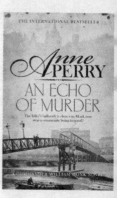

GO TO WWW.ANNEPERRY.CO.UK
TO FIND OUT MORE

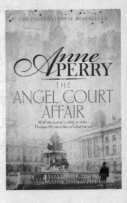

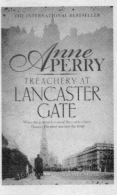

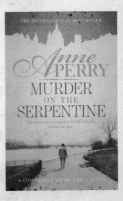

THRILLINGLY GOOD BOOKS
FROM CRIMINALLY
GOOD WRITERS

CRIME SCENE GRIPPING

CRIME
FILES

CRIME FILES BRINGS YOU THE LATEST RELEASES FROM TOP CRIME AND THRILLER AUTHORS.

SIGN UP ONLINE FOR OUR MONTHLY NEWSLETTER AND BE THE FIRST TO KNOW ABOUT OUR COMPETITIONS, NEW BOOKS AND MORE.